M.V. Maddux

Shadows to Light

M.V. Maddux

2019

Dedication

To Rachel Maddux,

my aunt and a true inspiration

"Darkness cannot drive out darkness;

only light can do that.

Hate cannot drive out hate;

only love can do that."

Martin Luther King Jr.[1]

Part I: Homecoming

Chapter 1

Entering town, the stores and businesses were a mix of old and new with the old outnumbering the new. The new consisted of fast food chains: a Walmart, a Lowe's, and gas station food marts. The old were dilapidated family businesses that were obviously just trying to survive.

A large sign welcoming visitors stood on the side of the road: CARBON, POPULATION 14,769. Places of interest were listed underneath. I couldn't help but wonder who exactly would be interested in those places. The list hadn't gotten any longer since the last time I'd been there, and the population hadn't changed much since I'd left in 1961. *Surviving, that's all it's doing. Glad I got out when I did.*

As I bumped over the railroad tracks on the north end of town, I had to smile. I was disappointed that my mother wasn't there to see me ride in on my hog. *God, would she detest the sight of me showing up in her town on a motorcycle.*

The north end of Carbon had never been considered the right side of town. But once you crossed the tracks heading south, the condition of the homes, buildings and businesses began to improve. Like most towns, the right side of town and the wrong side of town had great significance for those living there. It played out in schools, churches, and social circles.

Riding through, I passed the tallest structure in town, the Hartford Hotel. That building was thirteen stories high; I never understood how old man Hartford could justify constructing such a building in Carbon. The next tallest was the four-story Professional Building that used to house the local Rexall Drug, Sam's Barber Shop, Harry's Hat Shop, and Frank's Shoe Shop, all located on the ground floor. Lawyers, accountants, doctors, dentists, and even the local radio station offices had once occupied the upper floors. My heart sank as I saw vacancy after vacancy. The hotel's windows and doors were boarded up and so were many of the Professional Building's.

Most of the old department stores, pharmacies, hardware stores, car dealers, and banks were gone too. Those buildings had been taken over by used-book stores, consignment shops, flower shops, and t-shirt shops. The bars were still there though. It was reassuring to know that some of the old crowd must still be around.

I passed by the Majestic, one of the two theaters in town. It looked like it hadn't been open in years. The marquee read **CLOSED FOR RENOVATION**. I hoped it was true. I'd had a lot of fun there.

The smell of burgers and hot fries shifted my attention from the scenery to my stomach, a reminder that I was coming up on Barry's Café, but there was no time to stop. The call had been urgent. Death was imminent, and I didn't want to miss it. I leaned into the gas and watched the stripes on the road disappear one by one. I whizzed past buildings and empty lots until, there on the left, I saw my stepfather's accounting office. Ed had been dead for over fifteen years, but his name was still on the front door. Maybe some of those tax cheats he'd helped figured Ed could help them in the hereafter. He would've gotten a kick out of seeing his name on the door after all these years.

I continued down Main Street, riding past a number of offices I'd delivered to on my old paper route.

A little more than a minute or two later, I was out of downtown and into the college area. The hospital wasn't much farther. Just go to the mall, turn left, and go for a mile.

I'd filled up in Bradley, so I still had plenty of gas but decided to stop at the old Harbor station near the mall to top off anyway. Suddenly, the thought of what I was about to face made hurrying less appealing.

* * *

The Harbor station was a new Chevron and food mart. I pulled up next to the pump and killed the engine. Stark silence replaced the roar. Boy do I love loud pipes. I swung off the bike, rested it on its kickstand, and took a few steps, attempting to stretch the ache out of my legs. Long rides are always tough, and my over-fifty legs contributed to the stiffness. I took off my helmet, set it on the seat, and ran a hand through my hair before rubbing some blood back into my thighs. My leathers weren't exactly smooth. I looked at my helmet and chaps. *I think I must have killed every bug in southeastern Kansas. I must be some sight, bug guts everywhere. Oh well, I won't be wearing these much longer.* I hate helmet laws, but I would have eaten a pound of Kansas's bugs on that trip had it not been for that helmet.

As I removed the gas cap, I heard a "Hey!" behind me.

I swiveled my head to see what the trouble was. At first, I didn't recognize the man staring me down. He was older than me by at least twenty years and wore his hair in a short, military style. His hand rested on the handle of his gas pump, which was fueling a respectable-looking Ford pickup. I recognized him then. He was no one of particular significance to me, but you can't spend the bulk of your growing up years in a town like Carbon without know-ing people and them knowing you. This particular person used to spend his Sundays passing the collection plate at the Methodist church. He glared at my bike, my leather jacket and then at me.

"I know you," he said in the sort of haughty voice certain folks of the religious persuasion have mastered.

"Yeah?" I answered. "What about it?"

He snorted and the pump clicked off. He turned his back on me, jiggled free the last few drops, and returned the handle to its pump. "You're a lazy ingrate, that's what," he said. "You should be ashamed of yourself and the way you treated your parents."

He was already climbing back into his truck when I said, "Thank you. I'll be sure to take that into consideration." The guy ignored me and drove off.

"Asshole," I muttered.

I hadn't been in town for a full ten minutes before re-ceiving one true Carbon-style welcome home greeting. I couldn't wait to see what awaited me at the hospital.

* * *

It was just after 8:00 p.m. when I arrived at the Mt. Olive Hospital. For a regional hospital, its brick façade and hap-hazardly manicured green spaces weren't much to look at. Best I could tell, it'd been built in the 1930s.

I stowed the bug-crusted chaps and helmet on the bike. I still had my motorcycle boots, blue jeans with a Har-ley belt buckle, a black Harley shirt, and my bug-stained leather jacket on. At least the shirt didn't have naked wom-en and swear words on it. After combing my hair and put-ting some new snuff in my mouth, I was ready. There was nothing I could do about my pit stains and damp collar.

I thought I looked somewhat presentable but was sure I smelled like the last rose of summer. *Well, hell. It is August. Can't have everything.*

The lady at the information desk was distracted by something on her screen and didn't see me coming. Apparently didn't smell me either. "Excuse me," I said. "Can I get the room number of Mrs. Pearl Ellis, please?"

With a few keystrokes, she found what I needed. "Ellis. Three zero one five."

"Thanks," I replied and headed down the stained carpet hallway toward the elevator.

Third and top floor.

I passed several statues of saints, and every hallway had its requisite religious pictures and crucifixes hanging on the walls. The fact that Mom had to get treatment at a Catholic hospital always set her off.

My boots squeaked on the dull linoleum floors, but there wasn't anyone around to notice or care. The hospital may have been old, but it was definitely clean and orderly. Mom with her false preoccupation with humility and purity couldn't knock it on those counts at least. I counted down the room numbers but lost track of which one I was looking for. A paper nametag hanging from an open door caught my eye: **A. Williams.** For a reason I cannot explain, I looked inside.

The bed was empty. Maybe A. Williams had passed. Or was he out for tests? Or was he merely in the bathroom? Hopefully, I thought, I'll get to Mom's bed and similarly find it empty.

I wondered if I was too late. I wondered if I'd care.

Room 3015: P. Ellis. Keep walking, Max.

Up ahead, just past a steel cart full of used dinner trays, my cousin stepped out of a room and into the hall. *Room*

3015, I'd wager. She was followed by a squat nurse holding some charts and folders.

* * *

My chest tightened, and the chill of the AC couldn't stop me from starting to sweat again.

Claudia and the nurse exchanged a few words, but the nurse and her folders were already back at her workstation by the time I reached my cousin.

Claudia watched with a look of false affection as I approach. I nodded a greeting.

"I'm glad you're here," she said. "She's been waiting for you."

"I highly doubt that."

A familiar, frustrated look marched across Claudia's face, but she made no reply. Instead, she launched into a report of my mother's condition. It wasn't much different from when I'd spoken to Claudia forty-eight hours before, a conversation that ended with those three words everyone understands the true meaning of: "You'd better come."

As she detailed the end stages of chronic congestive heart failure, I stole a glance into room 3015.

The inner curtain was partially drawn revealing only blanketed feet at the bottom of the bed.

That was all it took.

My blood began to run hot. I did not hear Claudia's final words. I was too consumed by the hatred for those feet.

"Max!?" Claudia's voice jolted me back into the moment.

I looked at her and she did not smile.

"I said, since you're here I'll be going. I've been here all day."

"Mmm," was my only response.

An exasperated puff escaped Claudia's lips as she retreated into the enclave of 3015 and to a chair on the far side of the room from which she plucked a gray jacket and black purse.

I lingered in the hallway, watching as she stopped at the foot of the bed, placed one hand lovingly on those damned feet, and crooned to the top of the bed, "I'm going now, Pearlie, but I'll be back in the morning. Alright? You sleep tight."

I looked away. Saccharine nonsense. That's what it was. I wanted no part in it.

Claudia continued purring at my mother. Needing something to do, I removed my jacket. The creaking leather drowned out Claudia's voice, a bonus I'd not expected.

Moments later, she brushed past me, leaving without so much as a glance, which suited me fine.

* * *

As I entered the room and rounded the curtain, my mother was gradually unveiled: Legs. Torso. Arms covered in white tape and sprouting tubes.

She was sleeping. Or unconscious. Her hollow cheeks and dry, sagging skin bore all the signs of someone on death's door. Her mouth was wide open sucking in and exhaling air. Most notably, her eyes were open. I watched for a while. Those eyes did not blink. They just stared into space with not a flicker of recognition.

I looked at that wretched face and knew that soon I would never have to look at it again. I passed the bed without touching her, settled my sore body into a chair without uttering a word, and waited for that blessed moment to arrive and with it the closure I so much desired.

Shifting to get more comfortable, I posed a proposition. "Make you a deal, Mom. You don't talk, and I won't talk. That will assure that we don't get each other pissed off.

Let's also agree that there will be *no* touching. Okay?" I paused, then said, "I'll take that dead stare of yours as a yes. Thanks. I think I'm going to like this arrangement."

* * *

Pearlie Ellis was on her deathbed, and I didn't feel anything. I had wondered what that moment would feel like: Hatred? Anger? Love? Concern? When it came down to it, I didn't feel empathy, feelings of regret, nothing.

The closest I could get to a feeling was that of *the quicker you go, lady, the sooner it's over for me too.* I wanted to see dirt on that casket. I wanted to know she was gone. I wanted the whole past to be buried with her.

The old school clock on the wall said 9:02 p.m. Not late, but I was tired. Since Mom wasn't going to be a conversationalist, I settled back in my chair for some sleep. I'd figure out where to stay in the morning. I knew Mom didn't want me to stay at her house. Claudia had made that perfectly clear during our telephone conversation. She may have meant it as a jab, but I'd have rather slept under a bridge than in my mother's house. As dangerous as sleeping under a bridge may sound, I'd never been safe under my mother's roof.

I'd worry about a place to stay and all the other crap later. Right then all I wanted was to be on deathwatch.

And for one night, the chair wasn't bad at all. I needed some sleep and to get some strength back in my legs. I knew it wouldn't be easy getting through the next few days, but I could handle it.

By 9:30 p.m., I was out like a light.

Chapter 2

"Let's go. We need to get moving if we're going to make it to the train station on time," called my mother from the back door of my grandmother's house. Mom seemed excited.

Lissie was excited too and asked, "Aren't you excited to see your father, Max?" She handed me the football we'd been throwing and took my hand.

Of course, I was excited. This was a big day for me. Other kids had dads. Now I'd get to have one too. I wondered what he would look like. Was he tall? Would he like to have fun and laugh? And, most important, would I like him, and would he like me?

"Yes, ma'am!" I replied. Not only was I going to meet my dad, I was going to the Wichita train station. I had never been to a train station.

* * *

"Mom, is that his?" I asked, pointing to an incoming train.

"I don't know, Max. We'll have to see," she said.

The train slowed to a stop and its doors opened. The people got off, but Mom and Lissie didn't move.

"Is that one it?" I asked as another train rolled in.

"I don't know, Max. We'll have to see."

More people got off and on, but none of the men came over to us.

"Mom, is that his?" I asked, pointing to another incoming train.

"Max, I do not know. We'll have to see," Mom said, stepping slightly to the left and forward.

It wasn't.

"Mom, see that train coming? That's four. I counted four trains. Is that one his?"

"I *don't* know, Max. Wait and see." Her tone said to stop asking.

Finally, a train pulled in and slowed as it neared where we were standing. We could see into the windows. The train was full of soldiers.

"This is it," Lissie said, putting her hand on my shoulder. "This is it, Max. Watch for him now."

Someone who worked at the station opened a door and stood next to it, waiting. Other people I'd seen there waiting like we were started shuffling around and talking in loud voices. A boy ran a small metal car along the concrete platform near where we stood. I wished I had my wooden horse to play with, but I'd left it at home.

We shuffled toward the open door as passengers disembarked, made their way from the train, and came toward us. So many men in uniform, and they all looked the same. Most of them carried large, green duffle bags.

My mother shouted, "Victor!" and danced up and down on the balls of her feet. A man came over and they hugged. I tried to decide if he looked like the man in the picture Lissie kept on her mantle. The man in the picture wore a dark suit and had longer hair. This man had on a uniform and had short hair. I looked up at him to see if his eyes looked the same but couldn't see his face.

When the man finished hugging Mom, he hugged Lissie. I wondered if he was happy to see them because he didn't smile. Mom and Lissie were smiling though, so everything must be okay.

"Say hello to your father, Max," my mother instructed. She was still smiling. That smile seemed almost as foreign to me as the soldier who was looking down at me. I wasn't sure what to do now that I had his attention.

"Hello, sir," I said, sticking out my hand.

"Well, look how you've grown," he said.

"I'm four. I start kindergarten soon," I said, looking up at him and pulling my hand back.

He had no hug for me but tousled the hair on the top of my head. He and my mother turned and started walking. I followed, taking Lissie's hand. I went along gladly thinking about how large trains are and about the horse I had left at home.

So that was my father. That hadn't been such a big exciting day after all.

* * *

My dad's fork still sat beside his plate. He poured another drink.

"How's your mother doing?" Lissie asked my mother.

Without taking her eyes off my father, Mom answered my grandmother's question. "She's well, thank you."

"And she still owns that farm outside of Bradley?"

Mother nodded. "She lives in town, but she's looking for tenant farmers for the new season."

"No, she isn't," Dad piped up.

"Why, yes she is," Mom responded.

He pounded his chest with his forefinger. "I'll farm it!"

The women looked at him.

"You?" asked Mom.

"Why not? Aren't I good enough to be a farmer?"

I looked up at my mother. She seemed not to know what to say, and that didn't happen often.

"What about that engineering job you said you wanted?" she asked.

"I can't go back to office work now," he said, banging the table and making the silverware rattle. I jumped. I felt Lissie's arm wrap around me. I leaned toward her careful lest I catch my father's eye.

"I need to be outdoors. Active. I can't sit around all day."

"But ... see reason, Victor. You don't know anything about farming."

"I've been to college. Sure, I didn't graduate, but how many farmers have ever set foot in a college? What have you ever done, Pearlie? You don't know anything about anything." He lifted his drink to his lips and muttered, "Stupid bitch," before emptying the glass.

The rest of us around the table grew still as he got up to retrieve a bottle from the cupboard. Lissie gave me a squeeze around the shoulders. I looked up to find her smiling at me. "All done with dinner, Max?"

I nodded.

"Go in the living room," she said, picking up my plate. "I have something for you."

I wasted no time. I was eager to get out of the kitchen, and the living room held the promise of entertainment.

* * *

"You can ask her, can't you? She needs a tenant anyway. You'd think she'd want to help out her own daughter and son-in-law. And I'm a war veteran too." The distance between the kitchen and living rooms didn't do much to block their voices.

I stood in the living room next to Lissie's radio. It was a floor model taller than me with a faux wood case and brass dials. The glass panel in the center glowed yellow when it was turned on. The tuning dial was longer than my finger.

Lissie came in holding some sort of paper all rolled up. "Come here, Max."

"Can't I listen to Gangbusters?"

"It isn't on just yet. Come here. Look what I have for you."

I drew near, and she began unrolling the paper. It was a coloring page. She revealed a covered wagon and a cowboy and then said, "You hold this end."

I gingerly took the two corners offered. She continued to unroll it, walking backwards, and I stared at it in wonder. On and on it went until she was nearly across the room. There was a horse at the far end. I could barely make it out.

"Don't tell me I've had enough to drink," my father roared from the kitchen.

I flinched, gripping the paper too tightly and crumpling it in my grasp.

Lissie glanced in the direction of the kitchen, then back at me. "Hurry now. Set it down."

I stood still, held in place by the booming echo of my father's voice. She set her end of the page on the ground, and I followed suit. "Here." She grabbed a book from the end table and set it on one end to keep the paper from curling back up. I looked around for a book near my side but didn't see one. She took the green glass ashtray from the table and set it on my end. She quickly reached into her dress pocket and pulled out a new box of crayons and hurried back into the kitchen without saying anything else.

"Now settle down, son," Lissie said. "Let's enjoy our dinner. Tell us about Burma."

My father mumbled something. I held the box of crayons. I wanted to work on the horse, but that end was nearer to the kitchen and would've put me in my father's line of sight. I knelt and rearranged myself, so I was lying on my stomach. I selected the brown crayon and began with the wagon wheel, being careful to stay inside the lines.

* * *

The lights on the streets cast a pale glow as we drove home from dinner at Lissie's in the old Ford. It was dark when we pulled into the drive at our house. I held the coloring scroll and box of crayons. My parents said nothing.

* * *

I followed Mom and Dad into the house. Mom turned on enough lamps to see in the living room, but my father stumbled down the dark hall and disappeared into the bedroom. I held my new treasures close.

My mother steered me down the hall. I felt sick. I didn't want to go in after him and with her. Before we got to the bedroom door, she turned me into the playroom. A bed and dresser with my clothes were there, as they always were, but I called it the playroom because I only ever played in there.

"You'll sleep here from now on, Max."

I stood in the center of the room and looked at my mother questioningly. She turned and closed the door without explanation. She must have gone into the bedroom next because I heard that door close too. The low murmur of voices came through the wall, my mother's deep voice and my father's even deeper one, strange and heavy.

I looked around the room. My father had come home from the war, and this room had become mine. I heard my father's voice and thought this room would be a place where I'd be safe. This would be my little fortress within the dark bowels of this house.

I carefully placed my scroll and the coloring box on top of the dresser. Looking at my toy box, I thought, Maybe tomorrow I'll get to go through Dad's green duffle bag and look for war souvenirs to show my friends. They'll love that.

Leaving the light on, I crawled into bed alone and fully clothed and fell asleep.

* * *

Shuffling feet and a bright light from the hallway woke me as a night orderly entered the room and checked Mom's vitals. My sore legs reminded me that I'd come a long way. I shifted in the chair, tucked my coat under my head, and closed my eyes.

Chapter 3

I had finished with the chickens and was nearly done watering the garden and longing for lunch when mother came around the corner.

"Max, get over here! I told you feed the chickens and the pigs. The pigs are sitting here looking at me like I'm gonna feed 'em. What the hell is wrong with you?" Dad grabbed my shirt and pushed me forward. I almost spilled the box of eggs I was carrying. I braced myself, but Mom came around the corner before he could let his hand or boot fly.

"Victor, I didn't convince my mom that you're the man for the job and could handle her farm just to watch it fall to ruin!" My mom sure knew how to make an entrance, hands on hips and checkered dress flapping as she fast walked herself across the hardpan dirt.

"I can't do anything right by you, Pearl," Dad yelled back at her.

Tucked safely behind haphazardly stacked bales of hay, I watched, listened, and thought, I know the feeling; I can't do anything right by him either.

Mom, primed for a fight, kept going. "The corn is past time to cut. You think you're a big man soldier, but you're lazy. Lazy!"

She hadn't even mentioned the dry ditches and unturned alfalfa. Even I knew better than that.

"Listen, you stupid bitch. You think you're so smart, better than me. You're nothing."

He swung around and headed in my direction. Before he caught me spying, I ran toward the garden and started watering. That was another one of my chores, so I'd probably be safe if he saw me. I liked watering the garden. My heart slowed down a little. Mom was still watching Dad. He was muttering under his breath and watching his feet, but it looked like the worst was over. My stomach reminded me what time it was. I snuck a ripe cherry tomato off a plant and popped it into my mouth.

Before the heat and pain registered on the side of my face, I hit the ground. I felt something warm burst in my mouth. I couldn't tell if it was the tomato or blood. Dad just stared down at me, then turned and walked away. Mom closed the distance between where she'd been and where I was in about the same time it took Dad to close the distance between me and his truck.

He yanked open the door and swung up and in. I still didn't dare move. I could only see out of one eye. I wondered if Mom would put a steak on it and keep me home from school the next day like she'd done the last time.

"Headed for the bars or that whore Mrs. Foster, no doubt. On top of that you are a cattle thief. My mother's cattle! You're going to jail."

Mother screamed until Dad started the truck and barreled down the road.

Before the dust settled, she yanked me up by my right arm and said, "We're going into town to see Ma."

* * *

Ma Bess came out the front door as we pulled up. She took me inside and washed the dirt off my face with a cold washcloth. She and Mom sat on the porch while I played in the yard. I couldn't hear what they were saying, but Ma Bess was doing most of talking, and Mom didn't look very happy. She never talked back to her mom like she talked back to Dad.

24

That night, Ma Bess made us a special dinner. I wondered if we were going to live in Bradley from now on.

The one problem was Ma Bess's cooking. I loved that woman, but I think her taste buds had died. Her fried chicken was never fully cooked. That made no difference to my Mom. You still had to clean your plate.

I tried to fill my plate with green beans, mashed potatoes and gravy, and just a little half-raw chicken. If I did it right, I could cover the chicken with potatoes and gravy and get away without eating much of it.

"Max, clean your plate."

Mom had eagle eyes. I couldn't fool her, but I knew that a dinner of fried chicken always included dessert. The usual was lemon pie. Ma Bess could make a mean lemon pie. I cleaned my plate.

After dark, Mom loaded me up in the car, and we headed back to the farm. Ma Bess followed us home. I didn't want my dad to be there when we got back, but I didn't want to be left alone with my mom either.

* * *

Ma Bess opened the door and went into the farmhouse. Mom followed Ma. And I followed Mom. The smell of pee was almost overwhelming.

"Victor, get up," Ma Bess said, nudging him with the toe of her shoe.

He opened one eye, looked at us, and closed it again. The kitchen reeked of whiskey.

"What's she doing here?" he said. I figured he was talking to Mom, not me.

No one said anything for a while.

Ma Bess folded her arms and looked down at the heap in the middle of her farmhouse kitchen. "We need to talk about the tax bill. It's overdue."

"I'll handle it," Dad said without opening his eyes.

"It was due two weeks ago."

My father winched and practically growled before lifting his red face off the floor long enough to yell, "Get out of my house!"

I had been frozen in place, but that unstuck me. I headed for my room. Before I got there, I heard my mother ask him, "Where have you been?"

"None of your goddamned business."

A second later, I heard a car door slam and from the bathroom window watched Ma Bess drive away.

* * *

That did it for Mom. She packed up the car with me in it and we left. We drove for a long time and ended up in Hobart, Kansas, two castaways standing with our suitcases at my Aunt Edna's door.

Chapter 4

Another nurse and another vitals check. *How does any-one get any sleep in a hospital?* And what I'd thought was a comfortable chair definitely wasn't turning out to be the best option. *If I do this again, I'll see if they have a cot I can use,* I thought. *But tonight, I'm too tired to bother.* I thought about Aunt Edna and my cousin. *Claudia used to be so sweet. I wonder what happened to her ... Oh yeah, my mother happened to her.*

* * *

I knelt on Aunt Edna's couch—which had doubled as my bed—and rested my chin on the back, staring out the window.

Claudia knelt next to me. She was a whole year younger but had been a novel playmate, though I flat refused to play tea with her dolls anymore. Together we spied on the scene unfolding on the front lawn.

My mother wore a plain wine-colored skirt and cream blouse. She had borrowed it from Aunt Edna. Mother did not own anything so nice. She'd worn the same outfit to each of the few job interviews she'd had over the past week.

In front of her stood my father. He, too, was dressed up. His suit made him look quite respectable. The two seemed like foreign objects, standing together in their nice clothes on Aunt Edna's immaculate lawn instead of in front of the ramshackle old farmhouse. Dad held a small bouquet of flowers and a package wrapped in brown paper, which he had tucked under his arm.

He looked contrite. She looked suspicious. He gave her the flowers and they headed for the house. Claudia and I scrambled off the couch and hid in the hall.

"Max," my mother called.

Claudia and I looked at each another. She elbowed me right in the ribs.

"Your mother's calling you," she whispered as if I didn't know.

I came around the corner. My mother sat in the flowered chair, and my father sat on the couch in the very spot I had just vacated.

"Well, come on over," he said. "Don't be shy. I have something for you."

He handed me the package. I unwrapped it. Inside was a die-cast car. A Ford with a shiny blue paint job.

"Thank you, sir."

He nodded and smiled. He was so different now from the man I knew as the weary soldier and the man in the picture on Lissie's mantle.

"Go on now and let us talk," Mother said.

I fled to Claudia's room, where we admired the car until my father summoned me an hour later, and he and Mom and I left together.

Looking out the backseat window I hoped that this was how things would be from now on, like my friends' families were. I rested against the glass and nodded off. We were all off to Wichita.

* * *

I tried to stretch the kinks out of my neck, back, and legs after spending the night in the hospital room chair. At least the nurses had let me sleep until 10:00 a.m. I stood and stretched my body and swiveled my neck. What a dreary room. The soft light of morning did nothing to improve its appearance. The light brown walls reminded me of something I wouldn't want to step in. Two thrift store–worthy easy chairs sat facing the foot of the bed. The single hospital bed with its metal frame and swing-out tray was old but functional. The TV mounted on the wall near where the wall met the ceiling looked almost as old as the bed. A private bathroom and small closet were close to the door on the opposite side of where I stood. The single window behind me provided a view of the sky and endless farmland, but, because the room was on the third floor, all you could see from the bed and chairs was sky.

The requisite medical devices stood by and hung over the hospital bed too. The wall-mounted heart monitor beeped incessantly. The IV stand had several bags hanging from it. I assumed that was where they dispensed medicines since Mom wasn't exactly in a state to cooperate, not that she would have anyway. The oxygen hose provided its breathing assistance from an outlet on the wall. On the bed hung the pee bag from her catheter, about a quarter full of dark, murky yellow fluid. I assumed that color of yellow was not a sign of health.

The one picture hung high on the wall opposite the head of the bed to ensure the patient could see and be comforted by it was of the pope talking to a group of young children, and over the door hung a very nice Catholic crucifix. I chuckled to myself. If Mom hadn't been in a coma, she would have had a fit about those decorations. *Well Mom, Mt. Olive is the only hospital in Carbon, and it's a Catholic hospital. Unbeknownst to you, there is probably a priest or a nun who comes in here and prays over you too. I'll bet they say Hail Marys too. They may even be planning your Last Rites right now.*

God, I hope she is somehow conscious enough to grasp some of this. What irony.

In addition to the sparse hospital décor were two small vases of flowers and one potted plant. I walked the few steps over the window sill and pulled the get-well card from each. They were from the usual suspects: one from her holy roller church, one from Mama Grace, and the third from Claudia. The one from Claudia was the biggest and brightest. *Typical. You never miss a chance to ingratiate yourself even with Mom lying here in an unconscious state, do you, Claudia?*

Where are those cards and flowers from all those ingrates that you always said owed you, Mom? You know, those folks you and Ed did things for to make them obligated to you. Doesn't work that way, does it? Didn't work with me, and it doesn't work with others. I can only hope you realize that now.

Being there in that room with Mom was eerie. It was the first time I had been alone with her in over ten years.

She looked awful. Her skin was a milky white, almost gray. She had aged so much. Maybe it's that she appeared to have lost a lot of weight. She was a tall woman who'd never been on the heavy side. Laying there even in such a small room and in a small bed, she somehow looked much smaller.

Mom had gone prematurely gray at twenty-one, but her hair was now snow white. When I looked closer, I could detect the veiny purple of her scalp. Even with her efforts to always appear "humble but clean" in her appearance, she would not like the way she looks today. Just the thought of that made every muscle in my body tense.

But the thing that bothered me most was her face.

It was basically the same face, but her mouth was now a large gaping hole. From this hole the loud sound of her breathing escaped like some portal into a place no one wants to go.

The most notable thing was her eyes. They just stayed wide open! They looked just like they had when I'd arrived the night before. They never closed, and it seemed that wherever I'd go in the room, those eyes followed me. I knew she was in a coma, but those eyes made me wonder what was going through her mind: Could she see me? Could she hear me? Could she understand? Part of me hoped she could. Another part of me couldn't stand the thought of another minute of her voyeurism.

Settle down, Max. This too shall pass.

She looked so helpless wrapped in blankets on that bed. She was motionless but all seeing, silent except for the deep in and out puffing of air from her mechanically assisted lungs.

I'm sure that any other son would feel sympathy. I felt none. I just wanted time to pass and the inevitable to occur. With that would come freedom and the end of my hatred. I could hardly wait.

I reminded myself that the next few days would be long. But with my attitude, they would not be full of remorse.

I told myself that in future days, I'd have to bring some reading material or something to break the boredom. As for right then, I sat back down, leaned back in my new favorite chair, and decided to take a nap.

As I got comfortable and closed my eyes, my body relaxed. I couldn't see her looking at me, and I figured that from where she lay, she could probably only see the top of my head and the ceiling—and the Pope.

* * *

"Victor, where are you?" Mom demanded. She gripped the phone so tight her knuckles went white.

"You get home now," she said.

The Lone Ranger was playing on the radio and blocked the noise from the other end.

"You will do no such a thing. I'll call the police."

She slammed the phone handle into its cradle and slapped her book down on the end table, then grabbed the phone again and dialed out.

"Lissie, your son just called and threatened to kill Max and me. He said he has a gun and is coming home to kill us! I just wanted you to know that I'm going to call the police."

"Yes, he's been drinking! He finished one bottle by noon and had started on another before he left and went who knows where."

They talked a little longer. Apparently, Lissie talked my mother out of calling the police.

When she got off the phone, my mother gathered me up off the floor, and we sat on the couch waiting for Dad to show. My heart was pounding, and my shirt stuck to the back of my neck. "Be calm, Max. Lissie is on her way. She'll know how to handle your dad. Just be calm."

Finally, the rumble of an engine drifted through the open window.

"I hope it's Lissie," I said into Mom's arm. She didn't move a muscle. After what seemed like minutes, the front door burst open and there stood a drunken, wobbly Victor swearing and waving a gun.

"I'm going to kill both of you fucking son of a bitches. Pearlie, you're a slut and you have made my life miserable. You make me sick."

I looked up at Mom's face. She didn't move.

"The kid is a pain in the ass too. I should never have married you, Pearl. What I've become is your fault, Pearlie. I'm going to get rid of you both, so I can have a life. I'm a war veteran; I shouldn't have to live this way. I deserve respect."

Heat and chills ran from my head to my fingertips. I stared straight ahead.

"Say your prayers, you two, or say whatever you want to say because you're both going to die!" He raised the gun and cocked it. He took a deep breath, stumbled toward us, and fell on his face.

Mom calmly stood, bent over his limp body, and picked up the gun. She paused for a moment or two looking at him before placing the gun on an end table.

"Max, help me get him to the couch."

We struggled, but we got him to the couch.

Lissie arrived a few minutes later.

"Pearl, get him some coffee," she said before directing her attention at me. "Max, you stay over there and give us some space."

I twisted the radio knob, trying to pick up the baseball Game of the Day with Dizzy Dean and Peewee Reese. I found what I was looking for: the St. Louis Cardinals, my favorite team. That was far more interesting than what was going on around me. I'd seen my dad passed out drunk too many times and my mom and his mom fussing over him so many times that game no longer interested me.

No sooner had I found my station than Victor bellowed, "Turn that fucking thing off. Can't you see I'm sick? I don't want any of your goddamned noises in here, Max!"

He rose part way off the couch and tried to take a swing at me.

As I jumped backwards, he fell off the couch onto his face. As he struggled to get up, blood trickled from his mouth.

"See what you made me do, you son of a bitch!"

He wiped the blood away with his shirt cuff, then his nose began to bleed too. Seeing that, he fell back onto the couch and yelled, "Pearlie, get your ass in here."

Mom came running. "What's the matter?"

She took one look at the blood, grabbed her apron, and began to clean his face. She was shaking. The color had drained from her face, and she lowered herself and knelt beside him on the floor. Gradually, she calmed him down and got him positioned properly on the couch.

"Victor, what caused this?" she asked.

"It's that damned kid and his radio. Shut him up and get him the hell out of here.

"I'll be okay. Just leave me alone and give me some peace and quiet," he demanded.

"Max, you heard your father. Go to your room. I'll call you for dinner."

* * *

When dinnertime came, Victor couldn't get off the couch without blood squirting from his nose and mouth.

"Max, scooch on to your room again now," Lissie said as she picked up my plate and put it in the sink.

As I headed up to my room, I heard my mother plead. "Victor, we should take you to the hospital and get this checked out."

"No way. All I need is for you to stop nagging at me."

Lissie called from the kitchen. "Pearl, what's going on?"

"Lissie, he's bleeding from his mouth and nose. He can't stand up without blood gushing from his face. I want him to go to the emergency room, but he won't go."

"Let's let him sober up a bit and see what happens."

"Okay, we'll monitor it. But Lissie, if it gets worse in an

hour or so I am going to call for an ambulance whether he likes it or not."

Now that was interesting. I planted myself just outside the living room where I could hear everything and watch my dad.

He would cough every once in a while, and the blood would ooze again. Mom got up from her chair across the room every few minutes and took note of the blood, dabbing it away.

After about an hour, she pleaded with him again to go to the emergency room. "Something is definitely wrong, Victor," she said. Turning to Lissie, she repeated, "Something is definitely wrong."

Lissie started to say something, but Dad interrupted her.

"Listen Pearlie, I'll tell you when I want to go to the doctor. Now get your ass out of here and leave me alone. While you're at it, bring me another drink. In fact, just bring me the bottle. Be quick about it too, damn it."

Brushing past Lissie, Mom stomped back to the kitchen and called for an ambulance.

An ambulance. Here at my house! What are the neighbor kids going to think? I could barely keep in my excitement.

A few minutes later, the sound of sirens broke the quiet. They were getting closer with each passing second. I sprinted for the door, hoping to be the first to greet them.

Victor stirred. "Pearlie, what the fuck have you done? Did you call the cops? I'll get you for this if it's the last thing I do. Pearlie, where the hell are you?"

Mother just stayed in the kitchen. Lissie was still at her son's side.

As the ambulance pulled up, I bolted out the door.

"Hi, son," the ambulance driver said as the second man began to gather several medical bags. These guys were very impressive in their all-white uniforms.

"Can you tell me what the problem is here?"

"Yes, sir. Um, my dad's there, and he's got blood coming out. He was on the floor. Now he got up. Well, my mom and grandma got him up on the couch. He's—"

"We'll go take a look and see if we can help him, son."

With that they rushed up the steps and barged into the house.

All I heard at first was a lot of swearing and screaming.

Several neighbors began to gather outside, wondering what was going on.

I wanted to see the action myself, so I went back inside and sat on the floor near the front door ready for a fast getaway if necessary.

"Sir, I need you to hold still," said one of the medics. One sleeve of his white uniform had a long red streak on it. Dad kept thrashing while Mother tried to hold him.

"He came in a few hours ago drunk as a—"

Dad took a swing but missed.

"You assholes have no right to be here. Get the fuck out of my house. I'll have you know I am a war veteran and deserve to be listened to. Get your goddamned hands off of me."

He used every swear word I knew on them.

"He's a heavy drinker. He's already downed two bottles of whiskey today, and I suspect he's got more in him," Mom continued.

"I figured whiskey was involved from the smell of the house and your husband's demeanor," said the medic still trying to hold my dad's arms down to take his pulse.

After a lot of wrestling and getting cussed at, they finished their assessment. Dad calmed down after a while or got too tired to fight anymore. After several minutes, one of the medics began to speak in a calm voice.

"Mr. Maddux, we believe you are in serious trouble. Your blood pressure is very high, and you have lost a significant amount of blood."

"Your blood pressure would be high too if two big gorillas burst into your house. You cocksuckers."

"Mr. Maddux, that kind of talk will do no one any good. We responded to a call for help, and we are duty bound to advise you of our findings and recommendations." He paused before continuing, "You are suffering from an unknown source of internal bleeding, probably brought on by your drinking."

"Oh, sure. My drinking. You sound just like that bitch I married. Get the fuck out of here."

"Mrs. Maddux, we suggest that you call someone to come over and watch your house. We need to take Mr. Maddux to the hospital."

"Hospital! I'll do no such fucking thing. I have my rights, you bastards!"

"Lissie, say something. Say something to your son. Talk some sense into him, please," Mom pleaded. She looked exhausted.

The medics made room as Lissie sat on the edge of the couch and laid her hand on his shoulder. "Son, just listen. You don't have to go anywhere if you don't want to right now but listen to these nice men."

"Mr. Maddux, the hospital is the place best equipped to help you. They have trained staff and doctors that can patch you up. Why don't you just come along with us? We'll assist you to the ambulance."

Lissie got up and moved out of the men's way.

The ambulance driver bent over to help Dad up. Dad's

eyes flashed, and he swung at the driver, barely missing him.

"I won't go any fucking place with you, you asshole."

The driver backed off. He turned to Mother and said, "We'll just give it a little time to see if he settles down. He seriously needs medical attention."

The women sat in the chairs. The men stood off to the side against the wall. I didn't move. We all watched and waited. For Dad's part, he went back to sleep on the couch.

A few minutes later, Mom went outside and talked to the neighbors who'd gathered on our front lawn. Mom's back was to me. I couldn't hear what was being said, but they all nodded soberly and several people hugged her.

In the house, the medics began to gather their materials and write their reports.

Dad continued to sleep. He coughed once in a while and blood again seeped from his mouth and nose. I saw Mom's apron on the floor, got up, picked it up, and bent over to wipe my father's face and then I just sat on the floor by the couch and waited for more blood to appear.

Half an hour or so later, I heard Mom and Lissie discussing things outside.

As Mom and Lissie came back in through the door, Dad roused. He heard their whispers and erupted.

"Goddamn it, Pearlie. Why'd you have to call my mother into this?"

"Now Victor," Lissie began. "These nice gentlemen want to take you to the hospital for some immediate care. I think that is a good idea, dear."

"Don't try to sweet-talk me, Mom. I am not going to any fucking hospital, and that is final. Now, will you all get the hell out of here, and that includes you, Mom."

Lissie flushed and stopped where she stood.

Dad sat up on the couch and struggled to his feet. I scrambled to move my legs before he stepped on or kicked me.

"If you fuckers won't leave, I will."

Suddenly, I was on my feet. Dad's fingers wrapped around my arm. His nails dug into the skin on the inside of my arm. He yanked me over to him and headed for the door. The ambulance driver stepped in front of us and leaned forward. Dad pushed the smaller man out of the way.

Once outside, Dad stumbled the short distance to our green 1946 Ford sedan. Opening the driver's door, he threw me across and into the passenger seat, then he fell into the car. The two ambulance medics were immediately at the car, hanging on to the open door. "Please, sir. Have some reason. Let the boy go. Don't do something you'll regret ... Sir!"

As Dad struggled to start the car, the ambulance driver ran to my side, opened the door, and yanked me out.

Dad spat blood out the open window, threw the car in reverse, and raced out of the driveway nearly hitting the ambulance.

He roared down the street past Mom, Lissie, and the gathering of neighbors.

Seconds later, a loud crash reverberated through the neighborhood. None of us moved at first.

After a moment, we all ran in the direction of the noise. At the end of the block was our car wrapped around a power pole.

To everyone's amazement, Dad climbed out of the car seemingly unhurt. He was yelling swear words and cursing the car.

After helping him back to the house and placing him back on the couch another discussion was had about going to the hospital.

Victor was calmer but still steadfastly refused to go to the hospital.

"Okay, Victor, what if your mom stays here with us tonight and she and I will watch over you until the morning," Mom suggested.

"But, should your condition worsen, you will go to the hospital," she continued.

Dad nodded and laid his head back down.

The medics again packed up their bags and prepared to leave. Before the driver left, he came over to me, knelt, put his hands on my shoulders, and asked, "How old are you, son?" "Seven, sir," I answered. The corners of his mouth turned up slightly. He ruffled my hair and said, "Take care of yourself, kid."

I smiled. I didn't but should have thanked him for saving my life.

Slowly the house calmed down. Mom and Lissie took places in the living room watching the man as he slept. No one said anything to me.

I found a spot on the floor near the couch, wrapped myself in a blanket, and watched too.

* * *

At close to 2 a.m., the sound of coughing and gagging woke us all. Dad sat almost straight up. Blood was running freely from his mouth and nose. He gasped to get a breath. His eyes were huge. He clawed at the couch, then at his chest. He was frantic. Blood was going everywhere. He gasped for air repeatedly, finally falling back on the couch.

Mom rushed over to take his pulse.

Lissie was screaming. "He's dead! He's dead! Tell me Pearl, is he dead?"

Slowly Mom turned around and nodded her head.

They both began to cry and hug each other.

I knew what dead meant. I had learned that lesson on the farm with animals. I knew Victor wouldn't be around. That didn't make me feel sad.

Somehow, I didn't need to cry. I did not understand why my grandmother and mom were crying. Victor had not been nice to any of us, and now he would not be around. That's all. No big deal. I was happy to have another story to tell at school, like the events of the last evening wouldn't have been enough.

Chapter 5

Two people entered Mom's room. The first was obviously a nurse. The second was her helper and was pulling along what looked to be some kind of laundry cart.

The nurse spoke first. "And who might you be? Are you a relative?"

"I'm Mrs. Ellis's son, Max," I said.

"Well, that's fine. I was wondering if she had any immediate family. You just keep your seat. We have some cleaning and straightening up to do. We'll be out of here in no time at all. Have to make your mom comfortable you know."

With that they went about their duties.

The nurse took all Mom's vitals. At least I think that is what she was doing. A lot of poking and prodding went on with the nurse constantly making notes on her clipboard.

The helper went about dusting and straightening the room. She also checked the bathroom to see if it needed service.

Then together they began to work on Mom's bedding. Expertly, they moved Mom around on the bed.

I watched with mild interest or perhaps just out of boredom as they maneuvered the blankets out from under and around her.

One of the women tugged the blanket with what looked like more force than intended, and there lay Mom fully exposed. Her hospital gown had gotten bunched up her chest and all the rest of her body lay there naked. Her boobs and everything, the catheter, everything was exposed.

At the sound of my gasp and the skidding of my chair underneath me, the nurse quickly reacted.

"So sorry, Mr. Ellis. We'll have your mom squared away real soon and be out of here."

My chest tightened and stomach clenched. That sight reminded me why I despised her.

* * *

The day after my dad's funeral, I came home from school and found my mother in the middle of the living room floor surrounded by boxes, albums, and pictures.

She was removing photos from an album and cutting them into pieces before tossing them into a trash bin. I watched as an old picture of my father was cut into half a dozen pieces. I glanced at the mantle. The framed photo of him was gone; only the white vase with blue flowers remained.

Mom looked up. Her eyes were like steel as they had been so many times looking at my father. She went back to her cutting. Snip, snip, snip.

I decided it best to leave her alone and headed to my room. I dumped my books on the bed. The first thing I noticed was my nightstand. Other than the lamp and clock, it was bare. I'd kept my army men there along with the coloring scroll Lissie had given me three years before. I'd almost finished coloring it long ago and didn't even unroll it to look at it anymore. But my heart leapt into my throat, and I started searching for my things. On the floor. Under the bed. On top of the dresser.

They were all empty. I kept looking. My Norman Rockwell picture of a little boy removing a thorn from his dog's paw still hung above the bed. I opened the top drawer of the dresser. Technically for socks and underwear, I'd also kept my marbles and favorite rocks in it. Empty. I pulled open each drawer in turn, the wood scraping as I opened and closed each. Empty. Empty. Empty. My baseball cards were gone too.

I opened the closet. A few items were neatly stacked up top. My puzzles and board games, even Candy Land—though half the cards were missing—were there, but the bottom of the closet had been cleaned out. The clothes rod was empty except for a few hangers.

I left the room with the closet door still hanging open. I went to the living room but lingered just at the entrance.

"Are we moving?" I asked.

My mother scowled without looking up. I wasn't sure if she was scowling at my question or the pictures she was destroying.

"Why would we be moving?"

"My stuff is gone."

"Oh that." Snip, snip. "Ma Bess is going to stay with us to help out. She'll be staying in your room."

A funny prickling feeling crawled up the back of my neck and down my arms. "Where will I sleep?"

"You'll sleep with me."

So many things had changed since Victor died. This was just the latest. I had lost my room, my solitude. We were going to go back like things were while he was away in the army. A chill ran down my back.

* * *

Sympathy for my mother? Concern for her dignity? No, I didn't have any. Revulsion is what I had. The end of this waking nightmare couldn't come soon enough for me.

* * *

After the nurse and her helper left, I tried settling back into the chair and to sleep again. No luck.

I spent the rest of the afternoon looking around the room and trying not to think of my naked mother and the memories that brought to mind.

I also did my best to avoid those ever-open eyes.

My efforts were futile.

By midafternoon I had had enough. Claudia would probably be coming back at some point, and I wanted to avoid her if I could.

I needed to check in with my old buddy Terry and his wife, Diana, to see if I could stay with them. I gathered my jacket and left the room, avoiding my mother's unseeing gaze.

Outside of the room, I paused and took a few deep breaths. I'd go back that evening I told myself. But for right now, I'd had enough. I'd made it through what I'd expected to be the worst part of the visit. I felt I had prepared myself for what remained. Only a few questions continued running through my head. *Mom, how could you have let all this happen? Why did you treat me like you did? Couldn't you see what you were doing to me and our relationship?*

The bitterness washed over me.

Part II: X Marks the Spot

Chapter 6

Riding the hog back through town was a nice change: sunshine, no wind, and about 85°F.

As I headed north on Main Street, the smell of sizzling beef and frying potatoes drew my attention again. Barry's Café. *Next time. I can't leave town without eating at Barry's at least once.*

I goosed the throttle and cruised past Barry's, then east on Fifth Street toward the edge of town past the Carbon Police Department. *Sgt. Lester would've loved my ride.* A twinge of sadness came over me. He'd been more of a father to me than my own dad was. He was a big guy, an ex-Marine who looked strong as an ox: big and barrel chested but with a ready laugh. "No weak, wimpy handshakes, Max. Make people know who you are. They won't forget a firm handshake." It became a contest each week to see who could crush the other's hand. Sometimes Sgt. Lester would let me win.

Our conversations always drifted to motorcycles. He rode a Harley-Davidson for the city and had one at home for personal use. Over the years, Sgt. Lester took me for several rides on the back of his hog. Mom never knew.

* * *

I rode out of town for about 2 miles until I saw it. The old farmhouse with a large barn with a big neon red X on the front. The sign at the road entrance said X Marks the Spot.

I pulled up to the front door of the barn. Only three cars were in the parking lot. The mix of classic rock and

47

country music greeted me as soon as I took off my helmet. I opened the door and stepped in.

The smell of stale beer and cigarettes greeted me. My eyes adjusted to the dim light, but I'd have been able to find my way in the dark. The pool tables and assortment of other games were all still in the same place. X always did feel like home.

I yelled, "Is this X Marks the Spot or what?"

Out of the kitchen came a very attractive woman about my age. "Who wants to know?"

Before I could answer, she yelled, "Max!" She ran toward me, wrapped her arms around me, and planted a kiss on my cheek.

"Terry, get out here and see who's here," she yelled over her shoulder while holding me close.

Terry hobbled around the corner.

"Well, I'll be damned. We've been wondering if you'd show up. How are you man?"

Terry Barnaby had been a best friend since the fifth grade. He'd taken me to Missouri to start hitchhiking the day I left home. I'd had a crush on Diana since grade nine, but she'd been Terry's girl for as long as I could remember. Now she was like a sister.

"Max, pull up a stool." Diana patted the bar with one hand and pulled a stool out with another. As I took a seat, she walked around the bar and started drawing a draft for me. Setting the beer on the bar in front of me, she leaned in and asked, "So, how's your mom?"

"I don't know a lot of details," I said, "Maybe I'll get to visit with the doc tonight or tomorrow. Claudia, my cousin, didn't share much other than Mom is terminal. From her appearance, I would agree. She looks like death warmed over. She has no color. She just lays there with her eyes open, staring into space. She never closes those eyes. It's like no matter where you go in that little room, she is staring at you. No sound either, just the air going in and out of her mouth. She looks very pathetic."

"Max, are you really going to stay till she dies?" Diana asked. "When Ed died, you arrived the morning of the funeral and left town that afternoon as soon as it was over."

"Yeah. I'm staying through the funeral. It probably doesn't sound good, but you guys know about my relationship with my parents. I want to see that coffin go in the ground, and I want to see it covered with dirt. I want assurance that all of this shit that's come down over the years is finally over."

"We may not know everything, but we know enough to understand where you are coming from," Diana said, tipping her head toward Terry.

"Is it positive that your mom is terminal?" Terry asked.

"Yes, of that I am sure."

Diana asked, "Are you staying at her house?"

"No. Claudia explained that I am not welcome there."

"Who the hell is she to tell you that?" Terry asked.

"She says Mom gave her instructions to not let me in the house. I believe her. That's perfectly okay with me. I don't have good memories of that place anyway. I wanted to ask you two if you might have room for an old friend for a few days."

"That would be wonderful, Max," Diana exclaimed.

"Sure buddy, love to have you. I may make you pour beer around here too," Terry said, laughing.

"Thanks, I'll take you up on it," I said before draining my glass.

"Are you going back to the hospital today?" Diana asked.

"Yeah, probably. But I want to relax for a while. I left before Claudia got there. I'm hoping I can time it right to miss her entirely today."

"So, Max, when was the last time you were in Carbon? Your stepdad's funeral I'm guessing?" Terry asked.

"Yeah. Ed. That son of a bitch! I've gotta tell ya, I'm not too broken up over any of this."

Diana handed me another beer and leaned in. "I knew you two weren't best buds, but I didn't realize you hated him so much."

"Oh God, yes," I replied. "Ed was Mom's disciplinary arm on many occasions. When Mom was pissed at me, she'd say, 'You just wait until your father gets home. There will be hell to pay.' Once, I was having breakfast at the kitchen table. I was 15 years old at the time. We all had our set places at the table; I sat with my back to the swinging door between the kitchen and the living room. As I was finishing my breakfast, Ed came through the swinging door and hit me in the side of my head with his fist. He said nothing and proceeded on to his seat at the table."

Diana flinched, and Terry just stared at me. I continued, "I said nothing. It hurt, but I wasn't going to let him know. I returned to eating. Mom looked on with a slight smile and look of approval. The next morning, the same thing happened. A fist to the side of the head. I figured that I had probably deserved the first punch, but two days in a row? I let it slide again and figured that was surely the last of it."

I paused, then went on. "Wrong. Mom was working on something over the sink when Ed entered the kitchen on the third morning. The punch to the side of my head came again. As Ed went to his seat, I yelled, 'What was that for?' 'Just general principles' he responded. I bounced out of my chair and reached across the table grabbing him by the throat with one hand while drawing back my other fist. He froze, and his eyes were as big as silver dollars." I laughed remembering how small he was and how big I was.

"Yeah, and …" Terry prompted.

"I wanted to hit him in the face, and he knew it. Before I could finish, Mom ran over with a skillet raised in her hand. 'Max! Don't even think about it. I'll crown you with this skillet! That is your father! Sit down right now and finish your breakfast,'" I stood imitating Mom and then Ed's face.

"Then I looked at Ed, not only were his eyes wide, he suddenly looked very pale. I let him go with a shove and left the house. I hadn't hit him, but I had put the fear of God in him. That was the last time Ed ever tried to discipline me."

"Wow, man. I didn't realize it was that bad. Why didn't you ever say anything?" asked Terry.

"I don't know. Just didn't know what to say, I guess. Besides, it's not like anyone could do anything. I just wanted out of here."

Terry and Diana and I drifted in and out of conversations for the next few hours as they tended to the bar and its customers.

I didn't say it, but I thought, it would have been nice to have had a father who cared instead of one who only did Mom's bidding. Ed was the opposite of my real dad, who wasn't a father either.

* * *

The day after Victor's funeral, the parade of neighbors, friends, and lost relatives began. I had never had so many hugs and kisses from old ladies in my life. The best part was that many of them brought food. Good food and desserts!

But the best part for me was the obituary. It was published in the *Wichita Beacon* on the Tuesday before the funeral. I read it with great interest and was thrilled to see my name in print listed as a survivor. I didn't realize it then, but "survivor" was the appropriate word.

I cut the obituary out of the paper. It was not a keepsake; it was something to show my friends. My name was in the paper!

The funeral was on a Wednesday. The attendees were mainly family. Mom made me dress up and told me to look and act sad. I followed her direction. Lissie was there, of course, bawling her eyes out. And Dad's two sisters, Erma and Rachel, came. They both lived out of town but came to the funeral with their husbands.

The minister said a lot of nice things about my dad and talked about the kind of man he had been. I was convinced the minister had never met him. There was no mention of Dad's drinking. They also did not mention a cause of death. I had heard Mom and Lissie saying the doctors thought Victor died from either an esophageal bleed or cirrhosis of the liver, both conditions brought on by alcoholism.

After the service, we went to the grave. The high point of the day for me was seeing the Army Honor Guard and the twenty-one-gun salute. After that, we all went to dinner. The adults made their small talk, and I was for the most part left alone. The only one who really talked to me was my aunt Rachel.

"Hello, Max," she said. "I'm sorry about what happened with your dad." I smiled and looked up at her. She had a soft face. I liked her instantly. "Hey, what do you say we go next door really quick and get you something to play with?" she said. I nodded. She took my hand and turned to Mom, "Pearl, I'm taking Max next door to the drug store.

We'll be back in a bit." Mom barely looked up. Rachel and I left the others at the restaurant and went next door. We spent a long time looking through the comics. She bought me a Superman and Batman comic book.

Rachel was the first Maddux family member that was fun to talk with. She was a great storyteller too. More than anything, she seemed interested in me. I vowed then that someday I would spend more time with her.

Your father dies, and all you remember is that he was an asshole and that by his dying you get your name in the paper, meet a fun aunt, and get a comic book. No sympathy, no tears, no real memories—not even a feeling of a void knowing he's gone.

* * *

I looked at my watch: 7:49 p.m. I'd managed to avoid going back to the hospital and told myself it was too late now anyway.

"Hey, buddy," I said to Terry as he passed me on his way to pour a drink for a customer. "I'm going to make room for a paying customer and turn in for the night. Diana already showed me the spare room, but where can I grab a towel?"

"Yeah, sure. Hall closet. Left of the bathroom door."

"Good night. Thanks again, man."

"Don't mention it. Hope you get some rest. Let us know if you need anything." He smiled and raised an empty glass in my direction.

Chapter 7

S howered and changed, I crawled into bed. My eyes and body were heavy, but I couldn't sleep.

* * *

After Dad's funeral, I couldn't figure out the best time to go to bed. Sometimes I went to bed early, before anyone, even before Mom and Ma Bess, so I could fall asleep before my mother came in. Sometimes I tried to stay up late. I hoped she'd go to bed and go to sleep first. This never seemed to happen.

I learned quickly enough that it didn't matter when I went to bed. In the end, my mother was still in there with me.

The night of the funeral, I beat her to the room and changed before she got there.

When I heard her footsteps coming down the hall, I huddled under the covers so far on my side of the bed I was nearly falling out. I kept my eyes closed and feigned sleep as she slowly unzipped her skirt. I tried not to move when I heard the dull thud of heavy fabric hitting the floor. I pinched my eyes closed tighter as I heard the familiar sounds of the rest of her clothing being removed. This was the same every night. What varied is what came next. I strained for the sound of her drawer opening. The drawer was where she kept her nightgowns. I didn't hear it.

The bed shook as she crawled in. My heart had already been pounding, but then I went cold as I turned just in time to see the sheets settling over her naked body. I tucked my face away, the image of her body floating behind my closed eyes like a reflection in darkened glass.

"Come here, Max."

Some nights I couldn't help but obey. Even though I wanted to get away. Even though I hated it and hated her and wanted it to stop. Some nights, like that night, I couldn't move—frozen in place and icy with fear.

"Max," she said, "you're the man of the house. You have to take care of me. Always remember, you must love your mother. Nothing is a higher duty for you than to love your mother."

I wished she would die.

As I did the things she told me to do, I wished I would die too.

I remembered my father's blank stare as the blood seeped out of his mouth and wished that image could be her.

I laid back in the bed Terry and Diana had given me and tried to focus instead on the sounds of clinking glass, muffled conversation, and billiards smacking into each other below me.

* * *

The smell of vinegar woke me. There was no escaping my mother's presence even here. I swung my legs out of bed and followed the smell downstairs. It was dark and quiet except for the hum of the dishwasher. *Vinegar for the glass so they won't spot. Of course.*

Passing the bathroom on my way back into my room, I had to check. No vinegar smell.

Growing up, the overwhelming odor in the bathroom was one of vinegar. Mom didn't like spots either, so we were never allowed to use the shower. It was baths only for all of us, but our bathroom was so much more.

* * *

"Max. Bathroom conference. Now."

I sat on the side of the tub. I knew the drill.

After closing the door, she opened the window, hiked up her skirt, pulled down her panties, and sat down on the pot as she pulled out a cigarette. She'd talk, and I'd try to block the sound of her voice and avoid looking at her.

I got to know that bathroom well. It had a single ceiling light, and the walls were covered in gray tiles. One large mirror was centered over the sink. The tub was a combination tub and shower. Since Mom wouldn't allow us to use the shower for fear of water-spotting the Formica shower walls, the sliding glass doors were unnecessary. But they were there. What was necessary was her one little smoking window.

Trying to avoid the smoke and the view, my eyes seemed always to be drawn to one special feature of that bathroom. Hanging on the showerhead was a red water bottle douchebag! Many were the times I would be getting an ass chewing and laughing inside as I stared at that douchebag.

Blowing smoke out the open window, she'd stand up, pull up her underpants, and flush the butt, waving her arms to move the smoke out of the bathroom before hosing herself down with perfume and opening the door. Ma Bess was never part of these convos nor was she ever anywhere near the bathroom when they happened. In a haze of nicotine and perfume, Mom would carry on.

* * *

All I wanted was some sleep. It was bad enough I had to deal with this stuff during the day. Couldn't I just have a few hours' peace? But no, the past continued to haunt me.

* * *

"Max. Where did these come from?" Mom yelled.

I looked up, startled. All I could get out was, "What is that?"

"You know damn well what these are. Where did they come from?"

I blinked and did my best to look innocent. I managed to say, "I don't know."

"You come with me, young man. We'll get to the bottom of this," she said.

She marched me into the bathroom and planted me on the side of the tub. The metal frame of the sliding glass doors dug into my butt. She took a deep breath and stared at me with those steely eyes. My mind flashed back to those days when Victor would punch me or throw me across the room. I was in for it, and I knew it.

Finally, Mom opened the window and sat down on the toilet. She lit a cigarette and puffed away. She sat for the longest time before speaking.

"These magazines are filth, and I am going to find out how you got them. You will tell me, Max. I found these in your treehouse. I know you and those friends of yours are in on this together. Where'd they come from? Who gave them to you?"

Again, the steely eyes flashed.

I wasn't about to tell her that my buddies Dave, Jerry, Stuart, and I had pooled our Christmas money and gone down to Rexall Drug to buy those girlie magazines.

"Nine-year-old boys are not supposed to see things like those magazines. There are laws about such things!"

The more she talked about the evils of naked women the more I thought about those nighttime antics of hers. Somehow those must be different. In bed, she always talked about me being the man of the house, having to take care of her, that I must love my mother, that it was my duty. Maybe that made her being naked not the same as those girls in the magazines.

"Sorry, Mom. It was just me. I swear. Those other guys don't even know. I was too embarrassed to show them."

"Take off your clothes, Max. Everything."

She took off her belt while I stripped.

She sat back down. "Lay across my lap. Now."

As usual, her swats hurt and could certainly raise a welt or two, but I didn't let myself cry. I wouldn't give her the satisfaction.

Spanking me wasn't enough. Mom went on a tirade. She took me down to the Rexall and demanded to speak with the manager.

"You can't sell this kind of filth to underage kids," she said, slamming the magazines on his desk. He just stared at her, then at me.

"I am the secretary to the chief of police, and if you don't take the appropriate action, I'm going to make this a police matter." She stared right at the manager until he broke.

"I'll find out who did this, ma'am, and fire them. You're absolutely right."

She seemed quite happy that some college kid was about to lose his job.

Chapter 8

"Well, good morning, sunshine," Diana said as I walked into the kitchen. "How'd you sleep?"

"Fine, thank you," I lied.

"Grab a plate and sit down," Diana said.

"Breakfast is almost done," called Terry from where he was standing in front of the stove. "I'm making my famous egg and potato scramble, and there's a stack of flapjacks on the table."

Diana and I sat down, and she looked right at me. "Max, yesterday when we were talking, I realized how little I know about you. So, if it's not prying, tell me more. How did your mom and Ed meet?"

"Sure. Why not? In a few days all this will be dead and buried. Might as well have the viewing now, eh?" I smiled, figuring maybe getting some of this stuff off my chest might help. My morbid humor landed, so I went on.

"Let's see, after my dad died, we stayed in Wichita. I think I told you that my mom's mom, Ma Bess, came to live with us and take care of me while Mom worked. Mom dated some guys off and on, I guess. But I never met any of them, and no one really talked about them. The first guy I met that I knew she was dating was Ed. Mr. Ellis himself. He lived here in Carbon and would come to Wichita on weekends to see Mom."

Terry interrupted to ask how hungry we were, then piled our plates high with the same amount of food all around and set them in front of us. *God, I love this guy.*

59

"From what I understand, Ed and Mom had known each other in high school in Bradley. I was told they had even dated some then. When he came back into the picture, he'd been married and divorced. He spent most of his time in Carbon working as a banker. However, he'd recently started his own business and delighted in telling us that he now had the largest accounting firm in southeastern Kansas: six people working for him. Mom told me he was also involved in a lot of civic organizations in Carbon: Kiwanis, Lions, Chamber of Commerce, Masons. The list went on. Mom said it like I should be impressed. All I knew was that Carbon did not have a semi-pro baseball team like Wichita had."

Terry laughed. "All you did care about when I first met you was baseball. That I do remember!"

"Well, Mom and Ed had their own way of crushing that dream—"

"Hey, back to story, boys. Max, what'd you think of him when you first met him?" Diana asked.

"Ed was … let's call him *a different type of guy*. As you know, he was a little guy, probably five feet, six inches tall. I was only in the fourth grade, but I was almost as tall as he was. Mom was five feet, eight inches tall. If she wore heels when she was with him, she looked like a giant. To see Ed with Mom made me think of the cartoon Mutt and Jeff."

"Ha!" Diana chuckled, then went on. "Yeah, that's the perfect way to describe them. You know, I always thought your mom was really pretty. I never could figure out how she ended up with Ed."

"Yeah, she did used to be pretty, I guess. She and Ma Bess both told me how Mom had won the Miss Bradley contest when she was eighteen. The way they made it sound, I thought that was as big as the Miss America Pageant. I don't think it's a big mystery how they ended up together. Mom had obviously had her fifteen minutes of fame and wanted more."

"Hmm," Terry said. Diana leaned in for more.

I continued. "Apparently, Pa Bill, Mom's dad was a big thing in Bradley. He owned the bank and the gas station. Both were very important businesses during the Depression years. Ma Bess and Pa Bill made it through the down times in good shape. Mom used to tell me that most of those people that remained in Bradley after the Depression owed their survival to Pa Bill in some way. Maybe that's why Mom liked Ed, he reminded her of her dad and the life she could have if she married someone like him."

"Makes sense," Terry said.

"Yeah. And my grandmother used to say sometimes that Mom was the apple of her dad's eye. Funny because I don't think Mom could claim to have been the apple of her mom's eye."

"What do you mean?" Diana asked.

"I don't know. I'm just talking. Just a feeling, I guess. Who knows. I was a dumb kid. But I loved that old lady— Ma Bess!"

"Anyway, Ed didn't give a shit about me, and he tried to be funny all of the time. Mom always laughed at his stories and jokes. I thought he was annoying. Ma Bess and I didn't get a lot of them, so we usually just sat there, but that didn't slow Ed down."

"So, how long did they date before they got married?" Diana asked.

"I don't know. A while. One day, Mom brought Ed home and announced that they were getting married and asked if I was excited. Ma Bess and I were dumbfounded. I could not figure out what to say, so I just asked if Ed was moving in with us. That was a poor but informative choice. My Mom said, 'Max, first you should not call Ed by his first name anymore. He will be your father when we get married. Your name will no longer be Maddux, as mine won't be either. We will be the Ellis family.' She was all smiles and sugar, coiling her arm around his arm and leaning in. It made me kind of sick, honestly. Then she said, 'Ed will not be moving in with us. We will be moving to Carbon to be with him. We will all be making a new start in a new town. This is the greatest thing that could happen to us. Aren't you excited Max?' It was a lot for me to digest. I wasn't excited but couldn't say so. Instead I asked, 'What about Ma Bess? Isn't she coming too?' Mom said, no, that my grandma would go back to her house in Bradley. I looked over at her and saw that she was trying not to cry. Nothing about that day made me happy."

* * *

There was one thing, but I couldn't tell Terry and Diana. Over that weekend, Ed and Mom had done their best to make me comfortable with the new situation. They told me I'd get to finish the school year in Wichita and then we would move to Carbon over the summer. I was assured that I would like the new school. It was smaller and had an excellent reputation, Mom had emphasized. As for friends, I would get to come back to Wichita and see my current friends during Ed's business trips. Mom also explained that because of Ed's business, she would not have to work any longer. She would be able to stay home with me every day.

That didn't make me feel better. Ma Bess and I had been doing fine, and I liked the limited time with my mother. It began to sink in that I was losing Ma Bess forever. I was losing the best mother I had.

They went on and on about our new home. Ed had rented a house. We would only be staying in that home for a short time though because he had purchased property and was going to build us a nice, large home with many bedrooms, a game room, and a huge yard on the best side of town in Carbon.

But the best thing I heard was that I would get my own room. *My own room. No more sleeping with Mom.* Immediately, I wondered if her nighttime antics with me would stop too. That alone could make the move worthwhile. I'd never told anyone about it. I was too ashamed. Somehow, I knew it wasn't right. I had watched my friends and their parents; none of the parents treated them the way Mom did me.

* * *

"I tell ya what day did make me happy," I said as I dug my fork into another pancake and dragged it onto my plate.

"Leaving her and Ed in the dust. And the best thing about it was how pissed they were."

Terry and Diana's mouths were full, and I was on a roll. It felt good to exorcise some of my demons, and mouthing off to a comatose version of my mother wasn't that satisfying. So, I kept going.

"Early on in high school, I began play a game with myself about how I was going to get out of their house and this town permanently. Initially, I thought that I would just escape. I had several pretty elaborate plots. I'd take my bike and ride away. I even plotted my escape routes. I'd sneak out of town at night and they wouldn't be able to track me. I'd hitch a ride from a trucker at the truck stop on the edge of town."

Diana put her fork down and laughed. "Now why doesn't that surprise me? Max, the analytic."

Terry smiled and nodded in agreement.

I finished off the last swig of my coffee and went on.

"I enjoyed thinking of the various schemes. There had to be a better life out there. I spent a lot of time planning where I would go and what I would do. I had almost three thousand dollars tucked away in the bank because I'd worked since I was in fifth grade, so I knew I could fund my escape. The bank account itself was the potential problem. Since I was a minor both Mom and Ed were listed on it. I wondered if they could stop me from withdrawing the money. I wondered if they could just take it all or if there was some kind of limit. At age eighteen, I could have their names removed. However, my plan was to be on the road prior to my eighteenth birthday. I had time to put together a good scheme. High school graduation was years away. But planning back then made it seem possible and gave me hope."

I paused and thought for a minute. Looking back, it amazed me how motivated I was and how I really had thought of everything.

Terry pushed his chair back from the table. "More coffee, Max? I'm going to grab another cup."

"Yeah. Thanks. I doubt I'll get coffee this good at the hospital."

Terry picked up Diana's cup too and headed toward the coffee maker.

He brought the mugs back and set them on the table before lowering himself into his chair.

"I've lived in Carbon my whole life," Diana said. "I can't imagine bolting like you did."

"It's not like I hated Carbon. It's that I knew if I stayed my mom would keep her claws in me. I *had* to get out," I replied.

"One of the things that'd been eating at me was that I just knew Mom and Ed would send the cops after me if I left before I turned eighteen. Because when we graduated, I was only seventeen. I figured she and Ed would call the cops and I'd get caught. Ed actually solved that problem for me, but anyway."

Diana stood. "You boys keep talking. I'm going to clear and wash these dishes," she said as she stacked our sticky plates.

"Transportation was my biggest issue. I really wanted a motorcycle—"

"That could not have gone over well with your mom!" Terry interjected.

"You're right, man. I knew that idea would be an issue to overcome. She had some relative or friend who'd been killed on a motorcycle, and she reminded me of that whenever motorcycles were discussed."

"And how'd that conversation go down?" Diana asked from the kitchen sink.

"I didn't lead with the motorcycle thing. I wasn't *stupid*." I laughed and continued.

"One evening shortly after the school year started, I brought up the subject at dinnertime. I started with, 'You know, I really need to do something about transportation for school and work.' Mom was quick with a response. 'Max, you have the use of the old Chevy when it's available.' 'I know, but Mom you need it during the day, and I need something during that time too,' I said. 'You're walking to work at Wilson's Department Store from school and then going to Ed's office to catch a ride after work now.

That seems to work just fine,' she responded. I just kept pushing."

"'It works okay,' I said. 'But I need something that is more flexible. I have the money in the bank. I think it's time I bought a car.'"

I could feel myself getting upset all over again. I was talking faster and faster.

"Then Ed piped up. 'A car! I suppose you want a Cadillac? You just want a car so you can cruise Main Street and chase girls like the other delinquents. What about gas and oil, and I suppose you will want me to pay for the insurance. Buy a car. That's bullshit!' I tried to appeal to Ed's businessman side. 'No, it isn't,' I told him. 'Several of the guys have cars. If I had one, I could haul others to and from school and make some money. I could make the car pay its way.'"

I took a breath before moving on.

"Mom wasn't buying it. 'Be reasonable, Max. A car is a needless expense. Your transportation needs are being met now. Besides, the money you have in the bank is for college, not for a car. You're going to need all your money and a lot more for dental school.'"

"Wait. Dental school? You wanted to be a dentist?" Diana asked as she sat back down with us.

"*No.* My mother wanted me to be a dentist. Dr. Maxwell Ellis. She was always going on and on about how much money they made and that they never worked a full day and lived on the best side of town. And—most important—people would call me 'doctor.'"

I could still hear her voice in my head: *With you as a dentist you will be able to take care of your mother. The Ellises will always be one of the most respected families in Carbon.* I wondered if I'd ever be rid of that voice.

"'Mom, you need to get off the dentist stuff,' I told her. 'You know I don't have the grades or the interest in being a dentist. There is no way I'll need money for dental school. I won't be going there.' That probably wasn't the wisest thing to say as it sent her into a tirade of the merits of becoming a dentist: the money they make, being called a doctor, the first in the Ellis family to be a doctor, the standing I would have in the community as a dentist, and on and on.'"

"Did you ever consider it, Max? She had some good points," Diana asked.

"No. Never considered it. I'd never let her buy me," I said.

"Buy you. What are you talking about?" Terry asked.

"What I mean is, she tried to buy everyone. She finished with a lecture about my grades. 'You can make the grades, Max. All you need is the commitment. We will help you with the expenses if you will just put forward the effort.' Then Ed had to chime in too, 'Yeah, get off your lard ass and do something in school. We've offered to pay you for grades, but all you do is just enough to get by. You are a disappointment, boy. You are acting like all the other dead ass kids in this town. No ambition, no drive, and no guts. All you want are things given to you.'"

I wondered if Terry or Diana had ever been accused by their parents of not having guts or drive.

"I tuned him out. I thought, 'Maybe I should grab him by the throat again. That would show him some guts.'" I smiled thinking about it. Terry and Diana must have had the same image in their minds because they smiled too: teenage me grabbing him and his eyes budging and his face going pale.

"Mom tried to end the conversation, but I continued. 'I have the money for a used car. I'm going to look around and see what I can find. If a car turns out to be too much, I'll bet I can find a motorcycle. I worked hard for that money, and I think I should have some transportation.' Ed laughed, 'A motorcycle! That would be great. A Hells Angel right here in Carbon. You could get a bunch of tattoos too. Get real. You're a joke, kid.' Of course, the real joke was Ed. Talk and jokes. That's all he ever was."

Terry nodded.

"Mom tried to shut down the conversation again by saying, 'I said there will be no car and definitely no motorcycle! Get those ideas out of your head.' I went into the merits of a cheap motorcycle anyway: costs to maintain, less gas, all that. I even brought up the motorcycle cops we had known in Wichita and Sgt. Lester. She really did shut me down then, 'Remember, your bank account is under Ed's and my name. We can stop your withdrawing of money at any time. All Ed needs to do is make a call. Get those car and motorcycle ideas out of your head.' I wasn't any closer to getting my vehicle situation solved, but I had learned something. They *would* try to control me through the money in my bank account. Can you imagine what they would have done if I'd stayed and become a doctor!?"

"They were quite a pair, your mom and Ed. Snooty bitch and the little man," Diana said.

"Ha! Yeah. One time on our way home from some awards thing or another we stopped at the A1 Grocery. The inside lights were on, but the exterior lights had been turned off. I could see inside where a clerk pushed a mop back and forth across the linoleum. 'They're closed,' I said when Ed turned off the car. He got out anyway. He stepped up to the door and pulled on the handle. Locked. He jiggled the door loudly then knocked on the glass for good measure. The guy looked up and waved Ed off. I heard the guy say something, but it was too muffled to make out. Then Ed started shaking the door again and hollered, 'What do you mean you're closed? Do you know who I am?' He pounded on the glass so hard it vibrated. 'Open this door!'"

Terry and Diana laughed, obviously seeing the scene play out in their minds.

"The guy scowled and used both hands to wave Ed off as he yelled back. That time I heard it just fine: 'We're closed!' Ed stormed to the car and slammed the door. 'I guess they don't need customers. I guess they don't need my business! I'll remember this.' 'The nerve,' my mother said."

"No way. Now you're making stuff up, man," Terry said. He leaned over and jabbed at my elbow with his coffee mug.

"No, man. I swear. That's how my parents were. One time, Mom and I were at that same A1. I was standing in line watching her plunk down items on the counter." I couldn't help myself, I had to mimic the way she picked up and placed each item with business-like precision. This amused Diana and Terry.

I continued, "The clerk was finishing up with the woman in front of us. He was a gangly teenager I'd seen in there before, but I don't remember his name. No, wait. Nathan. I think his name was Nathan. Does that sound familiar?"

"Not to me," Terry said.

"No. Doesn't ring any bells for me either," Diana said.

"Anyway. Nathan—let's call him Nathan—says, 'Good afternoon, Mrs. Ellis,' and started punching in the prices for our items. After he rung us up and the bag boy finished loading our cart, Mom pulled a small white envelope out of her purse."

I picked up a small folded napkin that was sitting on the table and held it out dramatically toward Diana and said in my best Pearl voice, "Now this," I paused for effect before continuing, "is to help some poor families with their groceries."

Another pause for effect.

"Nathan raised his eyebrows and looked at the envelope. 'Yes, Mrs. Ellis?' Then Mom said, 'Yes. It is Christmas time, and my husband, Ed Ellis, and I only want to help those less fortunate than us. But,' she said, holding up one finger, 'it is to go to a good Christian family. Do you understand, a Christian family?' Then she said, 'And be sure to tell me who gets it. My contact information is inside.' She handed him the envelope. He smiled and said, 'That's so kind of you, Mrs. Ellis.' 'Just doing my Christian duty. There's enough in there for two or three families. Be sure to tell me who they are,' Mom said. The clerk assured her he would and off we went. I knew better than to be impressed by her Christian charity."

I looked at the clock and decided I better be on my way. Besides, Terry and Diana would be wanting to open up the bar soon.

"Well, speaking of the queen, I'd better head over to the hospital."

Chapter 9

I wiped a fine layer of dust off my motorcycle seat and put on my helmet. The weather was perfect. I wished I could feel the breeze in my face and hear the wind in my ears. I needed something to distract me, something to drown out the noise.

The sound of my Harley only reminded me of my mom and how much I'd wanted to hit the open road, any road that led away from her and her town.

Mom had wanted me to be a dentist but finally gave up on that idea. Everyone else in town thought I had it made. Surely, I would end up owning Ed's business. To them it was just a matter of keeping my nose clean, but I was through relying on the Ellises for anything. I'd be on my own soon. That was my mission.

* * *

"Well, graduation is Thursday, and I want you two to know that I have made some decisions about my future."

"It's about time. You can't be sucking on the Ellis tit forever, Max," Ed said.

"Max, we have already discussed next steps for you. It will be college in Carbon next year, and you will major in accounting. Get those grades up and we can discuss going to a larger school in the future. Ed is going to give you some on-the-job training at his office this summer. Max, you are set."

"You know I'll be eighteen in November, and my future will be in my hands, not yours. I would like you both to listen to this because this *is* what is going to happen."

"To your comment, Ed. I have never willingly suckled on the Ellis tit, and I certainly will not be doing it in the future. To your comments, Mom. I will not be going to college in Carbon this fall, and I will not be working for Ed this summer. You two have made it crystal clear that whatever I have accomplished in my life is a result of your efforts, that the only reason I have succeeded at anything is because of the Ellis name, and that I am in debt to you both for everything up to now and for all things in the future.

"You should know that I disagree with you on everything you have said. I didn't ask for the Ellis name and would be happy to give it back anytime you want it. Also, I don't believe I owe either of you anything. My life is *my* life, and I intend to live it *my* way. So, as soon as graduation is over, I'm leaving. And I intend to stay gone."

Ed reacted first. "You ingrate. You're a loser and always will be. Look at all we have done for you, and you come out with this shit. Who do you think you are? I'm ready to disown you, you ungrateful little shit."

"Go right ahead. Do whatever you want," I said.

"Max, you listen to me. We will have no more of this, and you will do as we say. I will not have this," Mom said.

"Well, get used to it. I will be out of here next weekend," I responded.

Mom tried to get practical. "You have no money. You have no transportation. You have no place to go. Frankly, you don't have any skills to take care of yourself."

"You're wrong, Mom. You know I have money in my bank account. You and Ed can keep me from it for only a few months. I have socked a couple of hundred dollars away on my own for just this occasion. I have worked since the fifth grade. I know I can find work wherever I end up.

As to transportation, I plan on hitchhiking and when necessary use Greyhound. As to where I will go, I have been in touch with Tom Small. You remember him. We used to play baseball together. You'll probably also remember that he and his parents moved to Tennessee. They're in a small town just outside of Memphis. Tom says I can room with him for the summer, and he thinks I can get a construction job too. His dad is a foreman of the company and hires a few kids each summer. Tom is going to work there this summer and then go off to college this fall. Who knows, I might even take off with him."

Ed jumped in again. "God, you are full of shit. First, your mom and I will not give you the money from the bank. You'll have to run off with what little you may have socked away." He shifted in his chair and set down his paper. "Hitchhike. You'll be back with your tail between your legs by the second day. You do realize that you are underage. If you take off, all we have to do is tell the cops and they will go get you and bring you back. This is some crackpot idea you have boy."

"Yes, you can sic the cops on me, but you better be prepared to do it repeatedly. You can only bring me back until I turn eighteen. Do you really want to play that game?"

Mom jumped back in. "Listen, before this conversation gets out of hand, let's all just step back a minute. We have heard you Max, and you have heard our position. I would suggest we bring in a third party to mediate this dispute. Someone we all respect."

Oh boy. She is going to try to get me to go along with one of her stooges. Well, let's see what she does. It will make no difference to me. I'm out of here next weekend regardless.

"Max, I think we should ask Larry Graham to come by,

and we can discuss all of this and then all follow what he thinks," Mom said.

She seemed elated. "Max, I know you have enjoyed your association with Mr. Graham in DeMolay. I know his wife, and I believe they are good Christian folks. I'm sure he can talk some sense into you and make you see that Ed and I only want what is best for you. Ed, you call Larry and make the meeting happen, you hear?"

"Sure Pearlie, I'll make a call. But if I were Larry, I wouldn't want anything to do with this ungrateful little shit."

"Thanks, Ed. You are always so full of wisdom. Arrange whatever you want. In a week, I won't have to listen to your crap. I'll be on my own."

* * *

As usual Larry was dressed in his black suit and a white shirt and wearing a red, coffee-stained tie. The suit looked like he'd slept in it, but that was typical of Mr. Graham.

He held his large, black briefcase in one hand. I gave his other a solid handshake in greeting. I wasn't sure why he had a briefcase because all we were going to be doing was talking. The way he carried that briefcase looked like he would fall over if he hadn't had it.

He was eccentric, but I'd always enjoyed talking to him whether it was in his office while delivering papers or at DeMolay functions. That large unkempt man impressed me as being smart and wise.

Mom led us into the living room. Mr. Graham sat in the large chair facing the television, she and Ed sat on the couch, and I took a place on a straight-backed piano chair.

Mom began, "Larry, thank you so much for coming. As you may have guessed, we are having trouble with Max.

Knowing you have had contact with Max through DeMolay over the years and knowing you have the respect of both Ed and me, we thought you might be able to shed some light on our dilemma and be able to explain to Max why he is so wrong in his feelings."

Wow! This is going to be some fair hearing. Mom's already told Mr. Graham how wrong I am. I'll get through this though and I am leaving tomorrow. I can stand anything for the next twenty-four hours. Go for it, Mom!

For the next half hour, Mom and Ed explained what an ungrateful kid I was, how I had no appreciation for the name Ed had given me, how I owed them for all the things they had done for me, and, of course, that I was a general screw-up and needed them in my life to assure that I did not go astray.

I wasn't surprised at what I heard. In fact, I thought maybe it would give Mr. Graham a better idea of what my life was like with them.

Mr. Graham was attentive and made several notes as Mom and Ed spoke. He asked questions to make sure he understood their points. At no time did he argue with them or correct anything they said.

As Mom and Ed wound down the attack mode, Mr. Graham calmly said, "Max, I think I understand your parents' position. Now I would like to hear from you. I am not going to let you get interrupted. I just want to hear your perspective and understand what you want to do."

I did not want to get in a big argument with Mom and Ed on details of each of my grievances, so I decided to just present the facts as I saw them.

"Yes, sir. Let me just give you a list of where I am at:

"I will be eighteen in November. If for some reason I do not get out of here now, I will be gone in November.

"I do not owe my parents for the Ellis name. I didn't ask for the name change, and I would be happy to go back to Maddux.

"I also do not owe them for anything they have done for me. If the truth were to be known, they have hindered me more than helped me.

"I have worked since I was in the fifth grade and saved over three thousand dollars. My parents are listed on the account and have told me that if I try to withdraw it, they will close the account and take the money. That is not fair. It's my money.

"I graduated from high school last night. I am not going to go to college for a while. I will leave tomorrow by hitch-hiking. I know I can find work as I travel. I have a friend in Tennessee that I can stay with if I can get there.

"That is my list, sir. I don't want to argue. I just want to leave and be on my own. You have heard from my parents, and you have heard from me. I sincerely hope you can understand where I am coming from."

"Thank you, Max," Mr. Graham said. His permanently wrinkled brow didn't give anything away. He sat there for some time just reading his notes and thinking.

I was wondering if I should have gone further with my complaints. I could have gone into the sexual things Mom did, her almost daily sexual questions about me being "clean," and other items. I could have gone into the non-relationship that Ed and I had. I could have told Mr. Graham about grabbing Ed by the neck. *No. I'm glad I didn't mention those things.* I'm embarrassed by most of them. I didn't want Mr. Graham or anyone else to know about them.

It seemed like forever, but finally Mr. Graham began to speak.

"Well, Ed, you and Pearl asked me to participate in this discussion, so let me give you my honest assessment.

"You two must realize that you cannot make Max be grateful for a name, especially one he has no particular respect for. He also does not owe you for anything. Whatever you have done you have done as parents, and that comes without restriction. You must also realize that Max will be eighteen in November and an adult in the eyes of the law. At that time, he can go wherever he wants whenever he wants, and you will have no say. If Max were to leave now, as he has stated, you certainly would have the right to have him declared a runaway and make it a police matter to assure his return. From what I have heard, under those circumstances, Max would constantly be running away over the next six months.

"As to the money at issue. Max said he earned the money and placed it in the bank. Ed and Pearl, I did not hear you dispute that. Max, I am concerned that you might squander the money if it was all given to you now. Therefore, my suggestion is that you withdraw approximately fifteen hundred dollars, the remainder to be made available to you after you turn eighteen."

I felt a surge of energy and the thrill of victory.

Mr. Graham continued, "I'm sure it must appear that I am taking Max's side. That is not the case."

He continued, "Max, you have really drawn a line in the sand with your parents. You have made statements and accusations that your parents may not forgive or forget. You need to be aware of this. Based upon your statements, I believe that you should go to the bank today to get your money, pack up, and be gone in the morning.

"If you leave as I suggest, I would ask—no I would require—that you call home at least every two weeks. You need to be in control of your future, but your parents deserve to know that you are alive and where you are. Money will probably be tight for you, so call collect at least every two weeks.

"One last thing, Max. I say all of this because I know you, and I believe that you can make it. You need to go. You need to get out now. However, I do want you to know that I will lose all respect for you if you are back in Carbon in six months. Is that clear?"

"Yes sir," I said.

I was getting out for sure under my terms! What a day.

Mr. Graham stood up, gathered his briefcase, and said, "I think I'm done, and you folks have some work to do."

"Thank you, sir. I won't disappoint you," I blurted.

Mr. Graham smiled as he stood to leave, but Ed stopped him.

"Listen, Larry. I'm concerned about the little bastard running off and doing something, anything, that will cost Pearlie and me a fortune. You know he had that car wreck recently that could still be very costly. I've been looking into this matter, and I want you to draw up papers to declare him an emancipated minor. He doesn't want us; I don't want him. Draw it up Larry and bill me. Good riddance to him."

Mr. Graham gave me a look that said *I told you they wouldn't forget or forgive the things you said.* He nodded that he would do as Ed wished and made his way to the door.

* * *

I didn't know what an emancipated minor was. But if it was something Ed wanted, I knew it would be something that would probably piss me off. No matter, I was getting out before Mom could catch me in a moment of weakness and guilt me with her "love your mother" stuff.

She didn't love you. She bought you. And if she bought you, you were done.

Chapter 10

Claudia's voice echoed down the hallway as I neared Mom's room. Someone else, a nurse I guessed, was with her.

"Yes, just take care of Mrs. Ellis as I've instructed," Claudia said. "When her son finally gets here this morning—at least I assume he is coming to the hospital today—we will be having a talk with the doctor. I would assume that new nursing instructions will be coming out for you as a result of that meeting. So just go about your regular duties like I wasn't even here. I'll just sit here and read until Max arrives."

I toyed with the idea of going down to the coffee shop to kill some time to let Claudia get a little more upset. *No. Let's get this over.*

"Hi, Claudia," I said as I stepped into the room.

"Well, it's about time. I've been here since before seven a.m."

"Claudia, it's only a quarter to nine. I didn't know we were on a schedule. If you want me here at a certain time, all you have to do is tell me and we can discuss it. I do realize that you are the one who has had to do the heavy lifting so far. I'll do my best to help out. Just don't get on your high horse. We both need to maintain our best behavior for now. This will be over soon enough. Okay?"

"Okay," she said.

In an effort to say something nice, Claudia added, "You look much better today, Max."

I smiled. "Why thanks. It's amazing what sleep, a shower, and some clean clothes will do."

"Yes, but I see you're still wearing motorcycle boots and t-shirts. You will be wearing more appropriate clothing for the funeral, right? We will have a number of dignitaries there, and you can't just show up looking like a member of the Hells Angels."

"Claudia, just let me worry about my attire. I'll do my best not to embarrass you and the various *dignitaries*."

"Well, I'm glad we've had a chance to clear the air. This is hard enough for me. I don't need to worry about you and the presentation you'll make. I'm going to the coffee shop for a while. I'll be back before ten. Doctor Hodge is to drop by at that time. He indicated he wants to speak with both of us. You just stay here with your mom, Max."

"You bet, Claudia. Will do," I said as I mockingly saluted her.

Claudia sneered, turned on her designer heel, and was off down the hall.

Claudia is the daughter Mom should have had; they're a pair.

* * *

As Claudia left the room, I settled into my chair and scanned the room. Nothing had changed from yesterday. The morning sun was coming in the window and gave the room color and a sense of life, but Mom was still staring into space. The only sound was of her drawing air in and pushing it out. Her breathing seemed more labored.

I didn't need a doctor to come tell me she was dying and dying soon. *Next step, funeral. Then I'll be done with her and Ed for good.*

* * *

"Max, you need to come home right away," Mom said from the other end of the telephone line. "Ed had a massive heart attack … He's gone. Max, he's gone." Her voice broke. I could picture her face, a well-rehearsed combination of anguish and mock helplessness.

"When is the funeral, Mom?"

"Max, I haven't even left the hospital. You were the first person I called. I need you. Please come right away."

"I'm sorry, Mother, but I can't just drop everything and stay for who knows how long."

"Max—"

"Mom, call me when you have a date and time for the funeral."

"But, Max, I can't do this on my own. I need your—"

"Mom, Claudia is there. If you haven't called her already, I'm sure she's next on—"

"Max, I told you I called you first. Please come. You're my son. *Our son.*"

"Can't do it, Mom. I'll be there for the funeral. Have Claudia call me, so I can get a flight."

I could picture the scene already. Mom would put on a show. I wasn't about to be a player for any longer than I had to be. A few hours at a funeral was all I could take. I said my goodbyes and hung up.

* * *

When I pulled my rental car into the parking lot of the First Methodist Church, there were fewer than ten spaces left. I pulled into one as far away from the doors of the church as possible. The short walk and some fresh air would help me steel myself for what I'd find inside.

Like the parking lot, the sanctuary was packed. I recognized some of the people. It was easy to tell that, like the ones I knew, most of the rest were local businessmen and civic leaders.

As I looked at those in attendance, I thought of comments Ed had made about many of them.

I wonder how many of you know that the man you're mourning and honoring today hated you because he thought you inherited your wealth and positions. I wonder how many of you heard his not-so-subtle criticisms of some of the other people here. Did you wonder if he talked about you like that when your back was turned? Sure, his jokes and cryptic remarks made you laugh, but was he your friend? You could see that he wasn't a man of great physical stature, but could you see that he was truly a small man?

Inside, people were gathered around Mom. She wept almost uncontrollably.

When I approached, several people moved aside and went back to their seats. She reached out to hug me and motioned toward me. The remaining bystanders excused themselves, and we took our place on the front pew. The cold of the wood seeped into my body. Mom slipped her hand into mine and pulled it onto her lap. I pulled away. Undeterred, she slipped her arm through mine and leaned in. "Oh, Max. I'm so glad you're here. I know you wanted to come sooner, but I managed." I glanced sideways. *I told you straight up I wasn't coming sooner. Who are you trying to kid? And not a tear in your eye. But somehow you're pulling this off. You're good. You are very good.*

I tried to avoid making eye contact with her by scanning the front of the church. Ed's casket sat front and center not twenty feet away. I tried but it was impossible to avoid seeing it. The top of its open lid was within view no matter how I shifted positions when looking at the pastor, speakers, or singers.

"As we leave today celebrating the life of Ed Ellis, may we love one another and let Ed's life serve as a reminder of what it means to serve and be part of the community and body of Christ." Murmurs and the sound of rustling jackets and purse zippers rose as the pastor closed his Bible and stepped away from the pulpit.

Mother looked behind us at the people, many of whom were now turning to leave through the double doors at the back of the sanctuary. She rose quickly.

"Come, Max," Mom said in a voice loud enough to get people's attention as she pulled me toward the casket.

Leaning toward me, she said, "Come. Give your father a kiss and say goodbye."

"Absolutely not," I said, pulling away.

Mom shot me a look and smiled nervously as some of the attendees approached.

Well, you got people's attention. Not the way you were hoping, but you got it.

She closed the gap and once again slipped her arm around my elbow. "Max, stand over here with me. Stand with me and greet your father's mourners."

I uncoiled her arm from mine and moved far enough out of reach that her grasping would be obvious and embarrassing. "I'm not doing that either, Mom. You can manage on your own."

Images of the bodies I'd seen in Vietnam flashed into my mind. I didn't need to get that close to another one, particularly one I did not care for in life. Mom took her place by the casket as the higher-ranking attendees took their obligatory places in line to speak words of comfort and pay last respects. I passed them going in the opposite direction and stood at the back of the room watching.

* * *

In the parking lot, attendees milled about. The big Cadillac Mom had rented for the family to ride to the cemetery in sat in front of the main doors to the building. I half expected a red carpet. It seemed ostentatious to me, and the less time I spent with Mom and overwrought cousin Claudia, the better. Much to my mother's dismay, I drove my rental.

As the graveside service progressed, two thoughts kept going through my head.

First, I thought that with Ed's death the hate and contempt I felt for him would be gone forever. He was gone; therefore, I wouldn't have to deal with him again.

Second, I kept thinking, *I tried, you son of a bitch. I tried. If you would have done as much, we could have had a father-son relationship. It's your loss, Ed.*

As I turned to leave after the service, Mom grabbed me.

"Max, why are you leaving so soon? I need you. You should stay and help me adjust to my new life. What am I going to do without Ed? How can you just walk off and leave your mother?"

"Mom, it was a very nice funeral. Ed would have been proud. I need to get back to work, so I'm leaving now. As for you, you need to do a self-assessment. You have funds, a big house to live in, and a nice community that surrounds you. It seems to me that your big adjustment will be not to become a hermit. From what I have seen, most of the acquaintances that attended this funeral were here as a result of their contact with Ed, *not* because of their relationship with you. You need to enlarge your circle of friends. Go get involved in civic activities, church activities, or even school activities. Don't just hole up in that house. For once in your life, extend yourself and give freely."

"Oh Max, you know I already do those things. People just want to use me because of the money and position I have. What I want is for you to come back and take care of your mother."

"That's not going to happen. Never. I have a life and a family. I'm established, and I will not be taking you in. You are in Carbon for the duration. I sincerely hope that you can find a way to enjoy it and find your place within this community."

Without giving her time to argue, I was off to Kansas City to catch my plane home.

* * *

The machines in her room beeped and hissed as I remembered why I was in that hospital room.

Ed's death hadn't brought the relief from hate that I had anticipated. My disgust for him remained as strong that day in Mom's hospital room as it had been on the day he died.

I don't know how, but I'm going to have to handle Mom's death in a different way. Maybe by burying her and having Ed gone too, I'll be able to finally put all this hatred behind me.

I stretched my legs out in front of me, stared at the dingy ceiling tiles, and thought about Claudia's call and my true purpose for being here on this death watch.

* * *

"Max, she's not been doing well for a while. We talked about the fact that she'd need to go to a care facility," Claudia said.

"Mom's always said she doesn't want to ever go to a care home, Claudia. She's got more money than God. Hire people. What's the problem?"

"We did that, Max. Well, first, we reached out to some of the people your mom has helped over the years. People she'd been generous to. People she gave Christmas baskets and money to."

Right. Of course.

"We were surprised that when your mother's time of need came, those people weren't interested in lifting a finger."

"No surprise there. *Those people* didn't ask for her help. She was in it for herself."

"Max! You always assume the worse of her. I'm trying to fill you in here. Do you mind?"

"Go ahead."

"So then we hired people to come in, in shifts, older ladies. But your mom was in such a bad state. She just wasn't herself. She'd yell at them and accuse them of taking things from her. I think her mind was going because she said the most awful things sometimes."

Nothing new there, but it's not her mind that's the problem.

"There was constant turnover of staff, so I took over and managed the health care workers."

"I know you did. Thank you for that, Claudia. I do appreciate it."

"Well, you're welcome, Max. So, I hired people to provide essentially assisted living care within the home. They were running two to three shifts a day depending on the day of the week. But I just couldn't do it. Max, your mom's health has deteriorated to the point she had to be placed in Mt. Olive."

"Okay. Thank you again for handling that. Mom trusts you and sees you like a daughter. I'm sure she's grateful."

"That means a lot, Max. It's been really hard on me. When I first checked your mom in, she made a fuss about everything. Her room was too hot. Too cold. She hated the food. She told the staff they were too slow and weren't being attentive to her needs. Max, she was cursing like a sailor." Claudia paused, let out a sigh, then continued. "She called the nurses, orderlies, and even some of the doctors 'dumb shits,' 'assholes,' even 'worthless fuckers.'"

Pearlie, the news of your ungodly toilet mouth is out in the public now. I imagine the hospital staff is getting a kick out of your language.

"That's not like her at all, Max."

"You've got to be kidding me, Claudia. You and I both know that for all her holier than thouness, that's exactly who she is. Who are you trying to fool?"

"Max, people are right about you. Just get here now. You of all people need to come. You owe her that."

Well, Mom. You called in your favors and no one came. I'm the last one on your list. All that wasted time. You should've known better.

* * *

Claudia had done a lot for Mom, but Claudia's motives were as transparent as Mother's had always been.

* * *

Ed set down the sports section as Mom walked in the door. "How is your mom, Pearl?"

Mom peeled off her gloves and hung her coat on the rack by the door. "Not good. The doctors will not do surgery because of her age. She will need at least two transfusions. I'll be there every day, of course, but I have duties of my own, like a family to care for."

She pulled a roasted chicken out of the refrigerator, set it on the countertop, and opened a cabinet. From the neatly stacked cans, labels all facing out, she pulled what she needed, and closed the door.

"So, what are we supposed to do?" Ed asked. "You can't keep driving back and forth between Bradley and home every time her ulcer flairs. It's costing us a fortune in gas, not to mention the disruption."

"My mother's assets are significant," Mom responded. "But her health is poor, and I'm concerned that she will burn through a large portion of the money. We need to keep her in Bradley and see to it that we do not have to go to the expense of a care home."

My blood ran cold. I clenched my jaw and didn't say a word.

"Poor Ma's in there all alone right now, but I have to mother my own child, don't I?" Mom directed her question to me, but I kept my head down and my focus on my homework. She wasn't asking me anyway, and I knew what was coming. The same thing happened every time Ma Bess had a flareup and needed extra help.

Ed picked up the newspaper again while Mom finished prepping the casserole.

She placed it in the oven and retrieved some notes from her secretary desk in the living room, then sat down at the kitchen table to begin her calls.

"Hello?" she said to whomever answered the phone. "This is Mrs. Ed Ellis calling for Mrs. White."

"Good evening, Mrs. White. We spoke on the phone after last Christmas. You remember ... about the grocery money I gave you."

Mother paused.

"Yes, I'm sure you are. But now I need something from you in return. You see, my mother is ill and in the hospital. She needs people to keep her company when I'm not there. She detests hospitals, you see. So, I need you to go down and sit with her."

My stomach clenched, and I tried focusing on my schoolwork. I had several algebra problems in front of me.

"I'm sure you are grateful, Mrs. White," my mother continued. "So, I don't see why this should be such a problem. My husband and I gave out of the Christian goodness from our hearts and now this small favor in return seems to be too much for you? I must say, I am shocked."

More silence.

"Well," my mother said, the satisfied tone in her voice palpable from across the table. "I should think it a small thing to do in return. Yes. I agree. You may sit with her tomorrow night. Starting about five? I'll need to get home to feed my family then ... Alright, see you tomorrow night."

She hung up the phone, and I heard the scratching of her pen on paper. I realized that my own pencil had stopped, and I was scowling at the plant in the corner of the room.

She began another call, and each word she spoke to the unsuspecting benefactor of her Christian charity stirred up something in me like stirring up sludge at the bottom of a water bucket.

My mother's gasp interrupted my thoughts. "Well!"

I abandoned my work and turned my attention toward my mother. She was holding the receiver away from her ear and staring at it in shock.

She huffed and slammed the receiver down into the cradle so hard the bell inside issued a pitiful ring in response.

Ed sat there reading with no reaction.

"Tell me to stuff it! We'll see about that."

She made some furious notes on her papers. I turned back to my own work not bothering to suppress my smirk.

Christian charity my butt! Mom collects obligations.

When she'd collected a sufficient amount of payback, she moved the phone back to its home, put away her notebook and pencil, and pulled the casserole out of the oven.

When she served me, she said, "Remember what I'm doing for my mom. You've got to do the same thing for me, Max. You always do for your mother; you've got to love your mother."

* * *

Claudia crept into the room. "I'm back. Brought you some coffee," she said as if there was a baby sleeping in the bed.

"Thanks," I said. She handed me the paper cup. I pulled the cardboard cutout mug handles from the sidewalls more for something to do than for their usefulness and watched as Claudia quietly moved the other chair toward me and settled in. Her face told me her wheels were turning.

"Before the doctor comes in, I want to talk to you."

"Yeah. About what?" I said, taking a sip of the not-hot coffee. *She probably ordered mine when she got hers and let it sit for the last forty-five minutes.*

"Well, your mom and I did some talking over the past few weeks about how she wants things handled after she goes."

She looked down, smoothed her pant legs, and pushed her purse under the chair.

"How do you mean?"

"Oh, things like the funeral, her things, and ..." Mom's understudy wasn't as quick on her feet as her role model. *God, she's had at least an hour to rehearse this before saying it out loud to me. I expect better.*

"Money. You talked about her money." Now I was having fun. I wanted to see her squirm.

"Oh, well ... yes, but no ... I mean ... that's not what I was getting at."

I kept a straight face.

"Listen, Claudia. No need to fret. I'm sure you're in for

a hefty sum, and I'm not going to make a play for your part." I looked her right in the eyes. She was blank. I don't think this scenario had crossed her mind. She was out of her depth.

"I know Mom and Ed wrote me out of the will years ago," I continued.

"What? What are you talking about, Max? Your mom loved, I mean *loves* you. And—"

"Claudia, do you remember when I had to come back to Carbon for a few months before I shipped off to Vietnam?"

"Yes, I think so."

"Well, I stayed with Mom and Ed but worked for Ed to earn my keep."

"I didn't know that part, but—"

"Well, one night while playing janitor, I noticed my name on some papers in Ed's office. Ed was meticulous about his desk, never anything out of place. But that night, laying right out in the open was a document with the title *C. Edward Ellis's Last Will and Testament*. And laying on top of that was a note with my name scrawled on it.

"No subtlety there, eh? Ed had to have left this out for a purpose. I knew he had drawn up the papers for the emancipated minor thing years before, so I had no reason to expect I would be in his will."

"Wait. What minor thing?" Claudia asked, seeming genuinely confused this time.

"Oh, that's right. Most people in this town don't know, but before I left—because I wasn't yet eighteen but wanted out after graduation—Ed had the papers drawn up for me to be an emancipated minor. Basically, Mom and Ed divorced me."

"Max—" I headed off any argument Claudia may be trying to make.

"The papers—with *my name* on them—were laying there for me to see. He knew I would be cleaning his office that night. So, if he had placed that will there for me to see it, I was going to read it. It acknowledged that I'd been an emancipated minor. It went on with several supporting reasons and ultimately came to the bottom line. They left me one dollar. The one dollar, it explained, was so I could not challenge the will."

That man had no balls. He was chicken shit. Couldn't address things with me head on, so he had to leave me a note.

I went on. "The emancipated minor status was just one more thing. I didn't come back so I could fight you for inheritance, Claudia. I'm here solely to see Mom go. Peace will be my inheritance."

"Oh, Max! I had no idea ... I mean, I can't imagine ..." She paused dramatically, but no shock registered on her face.

Claudia, you're as mercenary as Mom. But don't worry. Your payday is close.

Someone rapped a knuckle twice on the door. It was exactly 10:00 a.m. "Coming in."

Claudia leaned in and whispered, "Don't worry, Max. I'll take care of you." She stood and turned, all smiles, to greet the silver-haired, large-and-in-charge Dr. Hodge and his orderly.

Chapter 11

Dr. Hodge didn't waste any time. Looking at me he said, "I assume you are the son?"

I stood and extended my hand. "Yes, Max Ellis," I said as I gripped and shook his hand.

"Claudia mentioned that you were coming. I'm glad you made it. I suppose Claudia told you of the purpose of this meeting, but let me recap. Mrs. Ellis is resting well, but not in good shape. Consistent with her living will, she is getting nourishment through her IV. She is comatose and not going to improve beyond what you see today. Her diagnosis is congestive heart failure."

"Did her smoking habit cause this?" I asked.

"Smoking? I was not aware that Mrs. Ellis smoked."

"Oh yes," I said. "She smoked like a chimney. She would try to cover it up. But when she dies, the Phillip Morris tobacco company will probably go out of business. She usually smoked in a bathroom, blowing the smoke out the window and flushing the butts."

Dr. Hodge smirked. "That explains a lot."

Claudia wasn't smiling.

Dr. Hodge continued. "That brings me to the point of this meeting. As next of kin, Max, I need to know your wishes. Your mother will not improve. She is being kept alive by the IV fluids she is receiving."

He paused before continuing. "Decisions need to be made. If the IV is removed, your mother will pass peacefully in probably the next seventy-two hours. If we continue the IV, she could last for weeks or months, the actual duration to be determined by how quickly her organs begin to shut down.

"What are your wishes?"

I looked at Claudia, but she avoided my glance.

It was now clear to me why Claudia had insisted that I come back before Mom died. Claudia wanted me in for this decision; she was uncomfortable making it. She had been quick to tell me that I was not welcome to stay in Mom's house, but she wanted me to be the one to pull the plug. *I wonder what other little gems Claudia has in store for me.*

"Doctor, thank you for laying out the options. Claudia has been much closer to Mom than me, but here are my thoughts. As you stated, she is not going to get better. Her quality of life is poor at best. She's eighty-seven years old. I believe the best way to go is to remove the IV. I honestly believe that is the choice she would make if she were able."

"We'll remove the IV immediately."

"It was nice to meet you, Max, and to see you again, Claudia, but I need to move along. Have a nice day."

With that, Dr. Hodge and his orderly were gone.

"Thank you for taking care of that," Claudia said. "I'm just too close to your mom to make that decision."

"Not a problem," I muttered.

Sure. Not a problem, Claudia. A sick feeling began to grow in the pit of my stomach. I had just signed my mother's death warrant. I had seen a lot of death in Vietnam, packed body bags, carried the wounded. Pulling the plug on my mom was different.

Claudia made a move toward her purse.

"I'll stay here until this evening. You can go, Claudia."

Without a word, she pulled on her jacket. I grabbed the hospital-logoed pad and matching pen from the unused tray table and wrote Terry and Diana's number on it.

"Here. I'm staying with my friends Terry and Diana. I'll be here or there if you need me. I'll leave this info with the hospital too." Claudia tucked the piece of paper into her purse, turned, and patted Mom's foot twice as she left the room.

* * *

About thirty minutes after the doctor left, a nurse came into the room and unceremoniously removed the IV from Mom's arm.

I had not touched my mother since I had arrived at the hospital. But as we sat there alone with no sound other than her breathing and her insistent open-eyed stare into space, I reached for the bed and touched her toes.

"Mom, I'm sorry to have to be the one to make the IV decision, but I truly believe you will be better off this way. My decision was made out of caring, not out of vengeance. I sincerely hope you understand that."

I didn't shed any tears just as I hadn't shed any for Ed. I wished I could feel more, but the hatred was still there. I desperately wanted it to go away.

I sat back in the chair. Questions. That's all I had. Questions.

Why? Why, Mom? Why? What drove you to be the way you were? Why did you take advantage of me? Why were you such a hypocrite?

My fury was deeply rooted in the sexual abuse, but there was more to it. *If I'm going to deal with this, I need to understand it in the whole. Why wasn't I able to move on after I left Carbon and got out from under her and Ed's roof?*

I sat there alone trying to deconstruct our past.

* * *

One day, Mom and I had had plans to take the bus to downtown Wichita to go to the department store. I pleaded to take my best friend, Ronnie Johnson, along. Finally, Mom relented, and she and I met Ronnie at the bus stop.

We took the red line from Hillside to Douglas Street and disembarked in front of the Rexall Drug store. The sidewalks weren't too busy, it being a Sunday afternoon. Immediately after stepping onto the sidewalk, I noticed a familiar woman walking across the street.

"Lissie!" I said. I hadn't seen her since my father's death.

I turned to Ronnie and said, "That's my grandma."

"Where?" came my mother's sharp reply.

I pointed and was just about to yell out to my grandmother when Mother shoved my arm down and stepped to the other side of me, blocking my view.

"Hurry up now," she said, wrapping her arm around my shoulders and pushing Ronnie and I along at a faster pace.

"But I want to say hello."

"No. We will have nothing to do with any of that family anymore."

"But—"

"Don't you dare talk back to me! We have no need for people such as that."

Ronnie and I were struggling to keep up with Mom as her long legs surged ahead. I was having trouble understanding why I couldn't talk to Lissie. She'd always been nice to me. What had she done that was so wrong?

Seeming to sense my feelings, Mom stopped and bent over to talk to me further.

I dared not ask her any more but broke into a run, so I could escape her embrace.

I stopped at the entrance to the Jones department store. We could just go shopping now and not discuss Lissie.

He said nothing, but I wondered what Ronnie was thinking about me not being allowed to say hello to my own grandmother.

* * *

"Mom, may I go to the library tomorrow to work on a project with a friend?" I asked after swallowing a forkful of meatloaf one evening at dinner.

"Who's the friend?" my mother asked. She looked up from her potatoes and looked me square in the eye.

"Mike Compton," I replied with a smile.

"We haven't met him yet, have we?"

"I don't think so."

"Where does he live?"

"Somewhere by the park."

"Is he a nice boy? How does he treat his mother?"

"I don't know. I've never been to his house or met his mother."

"What church does he go to?"

"I'm not sure."

"Now, Max," Mother said sternly, "Honestly, you must learn to be a proper judge of character. If we are to cultivate lives worthy of our Lord, does it not stand to reason we must surround ourselves with those who would feel the same and will encourage us in our endeavors? You must not be lax in your duties. What would happen if you mingled too much with the Southern Baptists? Or the Lutherans? Or, heaven forbid, the Catholics? Be civil, of course, but choose your friends wisely."

I listened without comment. I didn't mention that Mike was black. I'd already made the mistake of bringing home Ben Sailor, which prompted a discussion about the merits of segregation and Mother's dissatisfaction with the fact that they'd integrated Carbon schools just a year before we moved there. Ben and Mike had gone to the segregated Douglas Elementary School on the other side of town.

"Maybe he's one of those damn Hindus," Ed said. "Reincarnation wouldn't be so bad though." I suppressed a groan. I knew what was coming. "In the next life, I want to come back as a bra."

He guffawed, and Mother gave him an indulgent smile. "Oh, Ed."

"Mike Compton. That doesn't sound like a Hindu name," Mom said.

"No, Mom. Not Hindu."

"Well, better that than a darkie," she replied, then went back to moving the potatoes around on her plate.

Since she was at work when I went to the baseball diamond, she didn't know many of the boys I played with were black. I liked the kids; we were teammates. I just wouldn't tell her.

I tried to hide a lot of things.

* * *

I looked over at my mother's face. *What you didn't know couldn't hurt me, Mom.*

* * *

Grace DeLong was Ed's office manager and secretary. I liked visiting with Grace. She soon became a friend I could talk to about anything. We would discuss school things, girls, people in town. No subject was out of bounds. Grace was Ed's first hire when he opened his business. She was friendly to my parents, but Mom always talked down to her. To Mom, Grace was a just another "darkie." Grace reminded me of Ma Bess, and our talks reminded me of the great times I'd had in Wichita with my grandma. Before long, I started to refer to Grace as Mama Grace. I never said it around Mom and Ed and managed to keep the secret. But when opportunities presented themselves, Mom had a way of getting and controlling information.

* * *

"When is your essay due?" Mother asked.

"The topic is due Monday. I have a few weeks to work on the essay, I guess."

She set two cans of evaporated milk on the counter in front of the clerk and nodded her head. "Find out the due date, Max. We want to make sure you stay on task."

"Hmmhmm," I said preoccupied with the candy display in front of me.

"Max, I'd like you to write about alcoholism again. Its causes. Its cures. Most importantly, how to prevent it." She said each word like a sharp slap.

My eyes snapped from the candy display to her.

She hadn't been happy with the previous paper I'd written on alcoholism. She looked at me sternly as if I had it in my mind to become an alcoholic and was determined to kill that notion.

Mike Compton was doing his research essay on the ancient Romans. That sounded more interesting to me than the cures and preventions of alcoholism. But I wasn't that excited about writing an essay about anything, so perhaps this wasn't a battle worth fighting.

"May I have a PAYDAY?" I asked.

She reached into the basket for the bananas and put the bunch on the counter before looking at the display.

"Please?" I remembered to say.

"Were you listening, Max?"

I nodded. "My topic is alcoholism." I tried to look obedient and neutral. She assessed me, searching for some hidden thought or emotion, but I kept those tucked out of sight.

"Good afternoon, Mrs. Ellis," the clerk said. He'd finished with the other woman and began punching in the prices for our items.

My mother gave me a satisfied nod, then looked at the clerk. "Good afternoon. We'd like a PAYDAY candy bar too, please."

At the car, Mother finished unloading the cart as she continued itemizing the merits of writing on such an important topic. I fingered the paper wrapping of the candy bar only half listening.

* * *

I stood and headed for the door. "Sorry, Mom. I need some fresh air, and it doesn't appear you're going anywhere tonight," I said.

On the way back to X Marks the Spot, I passed the Carbon City Kansas Community College. *The only thing that looks alive in this town. Maybe it'll save Carbon like college saved me—eventually.* My mind drifted back to the day I left Carbon.

* * *

"You know you're breaking your mother's heart, don't you, Max?" Ed asked.

"That shouldn't be the case. I'm just taking off on my own. This was going to happen at some point, and I think this is the right time in my life," I responded.

"You're an ingrate, son. And you are an asshole for treating your parents like this. You'll learn the hard way that

101

you don't shit on those who have provided you so much. You should be looking for ways to repay those you owe. You'll find out, boy! You'll be coming back with your tail between your legs. That will be a day I will enjoy. Just so you know, I am going through with the emancipated minor papers. You want to be on your own? Well, this takes care of that. You're free, boy. And we are free of you."

"Ed, thank you for those words of encouragement. I will do my best to live up to them. But don't count on me coming back with my tail between my legs. I'll do okay, and someday you will have to eat your words."

I left the house and caught a ride out of town with Terry. He took me as far as his work. I hitchhiked from there.

My last hitched ride dropped me at the truck stop just outside Memphis. I made my way inside and took out my wallet for Tom's number and went to find a pay phone. The first two times I called there was no answer. On the third time, about 5:00 p.m., Tom's mother, Sheila, picked up. We talked for a while and then she told me that it would be about 6:30 before they would be able to come get me. I thanked her and looked around for a place to grab a burger and some fries.

It was time to celebrate. I had made it! I had completed the first leg of my journey. *Stick it in your ass, Ed! I won't be coming back to you with my tail between my legs. I can do this!*

Tom and his family welcomed me into their hearts and three-bedroom home. As Tom's mom made an area for me in the basement, Tom asked, "You want to work construction too? Dad said he could get you on."

"You bet! That would be great. I need to make some money if I'm going to keep moving."

"Max, stick around for the summer and then you can go

over to Murfreesboro with me. Give us a couple of semesters, and we'll run that place."

"Sounds good to me."

As I laid in bed that night, I smiled. Not even a week out of Carbon, and I had made it four hundred miles, had a place to live, had a job, and a possible future at a college. *Not bad.*

No remorse. No homesickness. Just a feeling that my future was opening up. *Come on tomorrow!*

The job meant long, hot hours in the humidity, but rewarded me with large paychecks. Money that was safe from Mom and Ed.

One day toward the end of summer, Tom asked, "So, have you thought any more about coming with me to MTSU? You need to register soon if you're gonna go."

"Sure," I said. "I've got twelve hundred dollars in the bank. I think I can live on that for a while."

At the end of August, Tom's folks drove us to Murfreesboro.

As I recall this period in my life, I wonder how many of Carbon's college kids were like me back then.

I didn't take a full load, just three classes. Tom carried fourteen credits. I soon found out that I was not into schoolwork stuff. Liked the school part, just didn't care for the work part. Tom studied hard at every opportunity. Me, I was happy to hang around the Student Union Building. There was always a game of something to be had at the SUB. I attended my three classes for about a month, then quit going regularly. I was too busy playing pool for money. I was also making pretty good money playing hearts and poker. Those college kids were free with their money and not very good at cards or pool. Soon the SUB was where I spent every day.

One Friday in early November, Tom met me for lunch. His face said most of what he needed to say.

"Max, I'm pissed. I've had it," he said.

"What's the matter, buddy?"

"Don't give me that buddy shit. I never see you. You're always over here in the SUB. You know you're fucking up, don't you?"

He paused and went on when I didn't answer.

"I still don't know why you left Carbon, and I really don't want to know. But you are seriously fucking up, and you are not going to draw me into it."

"What have I done to *you*?" I replied.

"You've used me, you dumb shit. You've used me, and you've used my parents."

"My parents took you in, fed you, and gave you work. They didn't ask you for anything in return. I got you to come to MTSU with me. We were going to go to school and make something out of ourselves. All you do is sit in the SUB and play cards and pool. You're flunking out of school, you dumb ass."

I couldn't argue with that.

"You haven't even thanked anyone for what they have done for you. Not my parents. Not me. I'm headed home this weekend. I don't want you here when I get back. Go back to Carbon or go somewhere else … I don't care, just don't be here on Monday."

Tom got up from the table and left. I sat there dumbfounded. *Have I really been that bad? Am I using people? That's exactly what Mom and Ed did. Am I doing it too?*

I felt sick. Tom was right. I had used them. I had not properly thanked them for all they had done for me. I had treated them like I deserved such treatment. I certainly had taken advantage of Tom, and I didn't know how to repair it.

I called Tom's house in Memphis.

"Sheila, I just want to thank you for everything you and Senior have done for me. You took me in, and I really appreciate that you treated me like family. But … I think it's time for me to move on."

"You're welcome, Max. We wish you the best." She didn't try to talk me out of it. She must have talked to Tom already. I wrote a note and put it on Tom's dorm room door apologizing too. I wasn't sure if it would do any good, but I wanted him to know that I realized I had taken advantage of him and his family and that I was truly sorry. Deep down, I knew our friendship would never be the same.

* * *

Middle Tennessee State University, Kansas University, North Iowa Area Community College, El Camino College, Long Beach State, and The College of Idaho and New Mexico State University after Nam. Quite a winding route there, Max. But here you are. Wonder what old Tom would say if he knew how far you'd come.

MTSU—flunked out.

KU—same thing. Pool and cards.

Cut and run.

North Iowa. Not for me. Cut and run again.

El Camino. College number four. Made it through.

Got Cs, but Cs get degrees.

College number five. Long Beach. Two years out of Carbon and five schools. What a history …

* * *

I had heard that when people in Carbon would ask Ed what I was majoring in, his response was, "He's majoring in hall: study hall, pool hall and alcohol."

I clenched my jaw and goosed the throttle in an attempt to drown out Ed's voice in my head.

And then there was Miss DeBusk.

* * *

The wooden floors of the wide hallway creaked as I walked down it in my freshly shined dress shoes. The walls of The College of Idaho's Sterry Hall were covered with pictures of graduating classes, buildings, and benefactors past and present. I continued walking down the long corridor passing office after office until finally spotting a shingle hanging over a large oak door: **Dean of Students.**

After adjusting my new shirt and belt buckle and taking a few deep breaths, I opened the door.

"Good afternoon, sir. May I help you?" asked a good-looking, college-age secretary.

"Yes, my name is Max Ellis, and I have an appointment with Dean Binder."

"He is presently with someone. Please have a seat, and he will be with you as soon as he can."

"Thanks."

I sat in one of the straight-back, metal chairs with a cushion seat that lined one wall. I couldn't have felt more uncomfortable than when I was sitting in that chair. *This man is already pissed at me, and he's the one in control of my future.* The letter he sent me in Vietnam had shown what he thought of me. *How the hell did I get myself in this fix?*

A week ago, I was in Vietnam worried about rocket attacks. Now I'm sitting in a college reception area waiting for some dean I need to impress. I'm not above begging in this instance.

Damn.

"The Dean will see you now, Mr. Ellis," said the receptionist.

As I walked into his office, Dean Binder greeted me. "I assume you are Maxwell Ellis."

Without waiting for an answer, he motioned me to a chair. No shaking of hands, just a gesture to point at the chair I should use. Another straight-back metal chair. From where I sat, I could see only Dean Binder's large desk, leather upholstered executive chair, overstuffed bookcases—all hardback—and many diplomas. From his chair, he could see out a big window with views across the campus mall.

Family pictures and trophies were also placed strategically around the room.

Can he see how nervous I am? I doubt he even cares.

The large, middle-aged man with gray hair settled himself gracefully in his chair, leaned back, and looked me up and down.

I better not try to bullshit this guy.

"Well, Mr. Ellis, I believe from your letter you came to discuss the possibility of your entrance to the College of Idaho," he began.

"Yes sir."

"Your latest letter was written from Vietnam. When did you return to the U.S.?"

"I got home six days ago, sir."

"Well, let's begin. After receiving your application, I wrote you explaining that there had been an obvious oversight on your part. It seems you have attended a number of colleges in the past that you did not list on your application. You know, we receive a great number of applications each year. When we see errors like this, it is our experience that the applicant is attempting to cover something up. If it is not a cover-up, then it most often is just a straight attempt to lie in order to be admitted. I wonder if one of those scenarios fits in your case?"

No chitchat, just straight to the jugular. He must have been a cop in another life. I liked and respected cops, but this guy was definitely playing the bad cop role. I've gotta admit, he was good at it. I told myself it was time for the truth.

"Yes, I'm afraid I lied, sir." I attempted to say this with as much remorse as I can muster.

"I lied about the other schools because I wanted to start off with a clean slate. I left home right after high school. I hitchhiked, worked odd jobs, and used colleges like social networks rather than for learning. I spent the last four years in the service, and my time in Vietnam changed me." I paused.

When he didn't respond, I continued. "I'm sure you hear this all the time, but I really have grown up, and all I want now is a chance to start over and prove myself."

He said nothing. Just sat, cool, calm, and collected, and stared at me.

"I sincerely want to attend your school, sir."

For the next fifteen minutes or so, he lectured me about telling the truth. He went into the school's honor code and how my actions to date were a violation of that code. In all, he gave me a good old-fashioned ass chewing.

I made no attempt to correct him. I knew I was guilty. I sat there taking it and feeling my chances of getting into a good college slipping away with each word he spoke.

Finally, with the same cool, even tone he'd used the entire time, he said, "Mr. Ellis, because of your actions I am not sure what we can do for you. I have made my staff aware of your application. A final decision as to your eligibility will have to be made by our registrar, Miss DeBusk. I think it would be wise to go visit with her now. I'll ask my secretary to escort you to her office."

He stood and stuck his hand out across his desk. "Thank you for your interest in the college, and thank you for your honesty today. We'll see what Miss DeBusk has to say. Regardless, I wish you well in the future."

I got up and walked out of his office. *Well, that was a little piece of heaven. I'd better begin the search for another school tomorrow or think more seriously about reenlisting.*

I followed the good-looking secretary back down the long corridor. Finally, she stopped at another oak door with **Registrar** stenciled on it. She knocked and in we went.

The Dean's secretary addressed the woman at the desk. "Miss DeBusk, meet Mr. Max Ellis. Dean Binder asked that Mr. Ellis speak to you in regard to his application for admission to the college."

Miss DeBusk stood up and offered her hand. In a very deep voice she said, "Yes, I would be happy to speak to Mr. Ellis. I am aware of his application." She motioned me to a chair, and the secretary left.

Oh shit! Already aware of my application; I'm in for more of the same.

I took a seat in the same type of metal chair as before. *The college must have gotten a real deal on these.* This one made me just as uncomfortable as the others had.

I quickly tried to size up Miss DeBusk. When she stood up to greet me, I noted how tall she was. She had to be about 6 feet, 3 inches. She was an attractive lady with coal black hair. I guessed her to be in her early fifties. She looked like she was of American Indian heritage. Her voice was low and strong.

My guess was that in her previous life she had been a Marine drill instructor.

If I thought the Dean Binder talk had gone poorly, I guessed the next few minutes would probably be worse.

As I squirmed in the chair trying to find a comfortable position, Miss DeBusk thumbed through a large stack of paper. Finally, she pulled out several sheets, got up again, and came around and sat on the edge of the desk right in front of my chair. She laid the papers down on the flat surface, reached in her suit pocket, and pulled out a pack of cigarettes and a lighter.

God, the lady smokes Camels! Now I know she's a former drill sergeant.

She puffed on that Camel and looked over the papers for what seemed a long time before she spoke.

I wondered if she could see me beginning to sweat.

"Well, Mr. Ellis," she began. "I would imagine that Mr. Binder talked to you about your omissions on your entrance application?"

I nodded, trying to straighten up in the chair and look as in control as I could.

"The college does not take kindly to people lying to us. That is what you did, isn't it?"

Sensing that this again was not the time to try any bullshit, I said, "Yes."

"Please explain to me why you felt the need to lie."

As I had done with Dean Binder, I took the cue and began to explain myself. I had lied about the other schools because I wanted to start off with a clean slate.

"I am ashamed of my past record in college and didn't want anyone to know," I said.

"And my fiancée just graduated from this college. I've been paying attention, and I know that this school has a good reputation. What intrigues me the most about your school is the small teacher-to-student ratio. After being out of school for over six years, I know I'll need to go to a school where I could get some personal attention and not just be a number."

She stood, lit another Camel, then said, "You realize that you really shot yourself in the foot by lying."

"Yes, I know."

Miss DeBusk stood silently puffing on her cigarette for a while and finally said, "About all we could offer you is to start off on probation."

My heart skipped a beat. *There might be a chance!*

She went on. "If we were to allow you to start out on probation, you would have to prove yourself each and every semester. If you do not make your grades each semester, you will be out of here. Do you think you would be willing to take that risk?"

Without any thought, I said, "You bet!"

She crushed out her cigarette in the ashtray on her desk and perched back on the edge of the desk.

"Again, assuming we start you out on probation, what would you want to major in?"

"Gosh, I don't know. From where I was, I never let myself get that far in planning. But, if you were to let me in on probation, I would probably want to major in something general until I get those grades up."

She bent over from the desk until her face was about a foot from mine and barked, "General! You have all of that military training in electronics. Why wouldn't you major in engineering?"

Engineering! That thought had never crossed my mind.

"Ms. DeBusk," I stammered, "I've been out of school for six years. In high school I only took the easy classes, not math and sciences. From what you're saying, I'd be coming in on probation and competing with eighteen-year olds who've taken the proper classes while in high school. And besides, you are talking about me having to make the grades each semester or I'm out. A general major makes a lot more sense to me."

She took a drag on a new Camel and again bent toward me. In a stern, loud voice, she said, "You're chickenshit." Then she rose back up slowly, deliberately.

"*What* did you say?"

She bent forward again, blowing smoke in my face, and said, "You're chickenshit. You've had all of these life experiences, you've had electronics training in the service, you're a Vietnam vet, and you're chickenshit to try a challenging major."

After what seemed like a very long pause, she continued, "So, Mr. Ellis, here is what I have to offer you. We will allow you to enter our pre-engineering curriculum in January. You will enter on active probation. You must make at least a 2.0 in every class you take at this college, or you will be immediately dismissed. By the way, the grades you received at the other colleges will count toward your cumulative GPA. Your entering GPA will be 1.45. Those are the conditions of your enrollment at this school. Take it or leave it, Mr. Ellis."

She then sat back down on the desk, smoking and waiting for my answer.

This lady could piss off the pope. She just called me a chickenshit.

I didn't care if she was right; all I wanted to do was get back at her.

A major in engineering isn't what I was looking for, but I'll show this bitch.

"You got it, Miss DeBusk. I'll do it, and I'll invite you to my graduation," I said with conviction.

"Alright, Mr. Ellis. You will be hearing from the business office with the financial and enrollment details. Welcome to The College of Idaho."

We were done. I was left to find my own way to the door.

When I got outside, I had to run through everything again. I was accepted into the college of my choice. I was under the gun to perform by being on probation. I was going to start in just a few weeks. I was going to be an engineer. That last item was still a question mark in my mind.

The one thing I did know for sure was that I'd make that damned drill sergeant eat her words. No one was going to get away with calling me chickenshit.

"How are those grades, Max?" Miss DeBusk would ask every time she'd see me on campus. When I told her, she would just smile and walk away.

* * *

I pulled up to X Marks the Spot and headed inside for the night. *Max the electrical engineer who graduated with honors was about to drink some alcohol in a pool hall. Not much to say about me now, huh, Ed?*

Chapter 12

Mama Grace. What a sight for sore eyes.

"Young lady, there's nothing out that window but a bunch of wheat and cornfields," I said as I snuck up behind the woman who'd been more of a mother to me than my own.

The metal feet of the cafeteria chair scraped along the worn linoleum of the hospital cafeteria as she whirled around and smiled widely. "Max. Is that really you?"

Grace was an attractive woman of about seventy-five. As always, she was nicely dressed. The clothes she wore that day looked like her Sunday church clothes.

"You bet it is. You look great Mama Grace. What are you doing at the hospital this early … getting discharged?"

"No, silly," she said, waving her hand at me. She patted the table across from her.

I sat and smiled as her warmth enveloped me, chasing away, even if only for a moment, the chill I felt deep inside.

"I just stopped by to spend some time with your mom. I've been in her room for the last hour praying over her."

"You may have shortchanged her. I'm sure she needs more than an hour of prayer."

"Max, I know you're aware that this is not the time for such comments. She's at death's door and needs compassion and forgiveness." She looked right at me. I knew better than to argue.

"Now, Max, enough of that. Tell me about you and your family. Let's talk about happier things," she said as she flashed her big smile.

We discussed old times, and it felt like those long-ago afternoons when I'd go by Ed's office. Mama Grace and I would sit at her desk and talk about everything from life to baseball. She'd listened with such interest and asked so many questions—but not the ones my mother thought to ask. Mama Grace and I had also talked about difficult subjects. I could talk to Grace about my parents and often did. I never provided details, but she knew I didn't respect my mother. Even though she worked for Ed and personally held him in high regard, she was aware that Ed and I could not find a way to coexist.

After bringing her up to date on my life, I quizzed her about hers.

"Tell me about retirement. What are you doing, and how do you spend your days, Mama?"

"Oh, Max. I'm enjoying it. I spend a lot of time at my church. You know, I still lead the choir."

I pictured her like I'd seen her so many times and so many years before, at the front of the choir in her blue robe with the gold stole. The woman could sing.

She brought me back to the moment. "There are of many of my friends in failing health. I just don't have time to visit them all."

"Mama Grace, did Ed provide anything for your retirement?"

"No, not in terms of a monthly retirement check. But Ed always paid me well and let me work for him until he passed. I own my house, so I'm good. I get by, Max."

She must have seen the dark look I had tried to keep hidden.

"I don't have any family left, and my needs are simple. With my Social Security check, I get by just fine."

We sat in the cafeteria for some time discussing old

times. Not as active of a listener as Mama Grace, my mind kept wandering back to Ed and Mom and their treatment of her. It bothered me that such a fine lady was just getting by. *Ed could have done more for her. For that matter, Mom could have done more for her.* After all, Mom herself told me that Grace had continued to visit her regularly after Ed died. Mama Grace was one of the few who seem to have paid any attention to Mom. Those visits had to be out of compassion because Mom hadn't gone out of her way to be nice to Grace. Mom always referred to her as "hired help." Grace was so much more than hired help as evidenced by her early morning visit to Mom.

At one point, my mom had decided she wanted me to call her "mama" rather than "mom." I refused. I could never have disrespected Mama Grace that way.

"Okay, sugar. I should get going, and you should go see your mother." Mama stood slowly but gracefully. I hugged and kissed her, and we promised to get together again before I left.

I wonder if Mom thought of Mama Grace as a good Christian. If anyone is, I'd vote for Mama.

* * *

Standing in line for a cup of coffee before heading to Mom's room, I realized that Ed and I did agree on one thing. Ed adored Grace, and that didn't go over well with Mom.

Mom couldn't keep her nose out of Ed's business. She constantly rode herd on him. She'd tried to work on his projects just enough to always know what was going on in his business. Mom was quick to give her opinion about his employees and quiz him on their personal and private lives. Were they Christian? Where did they live? How did they treat their parents, particularly their mothers? Same old questions. But the one person Mom would never criticize directly was Mama Grace. Ed would always defend his office manager. Mama Grace was the only person Ed ever stood up for.

"Where have you been, Ed?" Mom demanded. "It's after eleven o'clock and you didn't even extend the courtesy of a phone call."

"I've been out, Pearl. Can't a man just go out every once in a while without having to get a kitchen pass?"

"Where were you?" she demanded again. She was stone cold.

"With Susan."

"Susan! You promised you wouldn't see her."

"No, Pearl. When we got married, you *forbade* me from seeing or talking to her. There's a big difference," Ed said as he sunk into the nearest chair.

He went on. "She's my daughter, Pearl. She called my office earlier today to let me know she was passing through town and invited me to meet after work at the Hartford to catch up. It was only supposed to be for a quick drink, but we lost track of time."

I sat there waiting. Neither one of them even looked at me.

"Ed, that is one of the worst things anyone has ever done to me. And coming from you! It's so disloyal…" She didn't shed a tear but watched Ed, who never looked up, for his reaction.

"The secrecy! It's a lie, Ed. A lie of omission is a lie nonetheless."

At least I know I'm getting out. Ed, you poor bastard. You're in it for a life sentence.

* * *

I paid for my coffee and walked down the hall.

Chapter 13

spent the rest of the morning in the chair I had grown to love in Mom's room.

Little had changed. The tubes and IVs were gone, but her eyes were still open with that empty stare. Her breathing was labored and even louder than before.

The duty nurse entered the room. When she noticed me, she gave me a broad smile. "How are you today, Mr. Ellis?" She was so damn chipper.

I cleared my throat. "I'm fine. There doesn't seem to be much change," I said. "With my mother that is."

The nurse nodded and assumed a somber countenance. "Yes. It can be hard to know how things will go in situations like this."

"I'm surprised she's hung on this long," I said.

"So am I, Mr. Ellis. I really am. I think she must be waiting for someone."

I considered that and could not come up with a list of possible candidates. Claudia had been there every evening. Mama Grace had been to see her. Ed was long gone. There weren't many other people in her life. There hadn't been for years.

I shrugged at the nurse. "There isn't anyone else."

After the nurse left, I leaned back and wondered. I sat there for a long time thinking about my talk with the nurse. Finally, I picked up a magazine and opened it but couldn't read.

I realized that I hadn't really directly spoken to Mom since coming back to see her, not spoken my mind. I looked at her open eyes. I had no idea if she could see me. Even less if she could hear me. I scowled thinking of all the things I would say if I knew she could hear. All the ways I'd knock her down one last time.

Somehow, they all seemed empty. I didn't want to take more cheap shots at her.

Maybe the nurse was right. Maybe she was waiting for something. Maybe she was waiting for me to say something nice to her, show her that I gave a damn, or just to acknowledge her.

After weighing the possibilities for some time, I reached out for her foot again.

"Mom, it's okay to go now. You do not need to put yourself through more misery. It's okay."

It felt good to say those words, but my body was still tight and there was an undefinable turbulence under the calm that had come over me. I milled around the room and corridor for a while before deciding to take a walk. I headed toward nearby Carbon High School.

By the time I hit the school's track, the cold shock of Mom's imminent death had morphed into a more familiar emotion.

As I ran through what was going to occur, my heart began pounding and my blood ran hot. I could not control how I truly felt: I wanted her dead. I wanted her gone. I wanted to be free of hate once and for all.

Why is she hanging on so long? Why isn't this over already?

After three or four laps, my pace slowed, and my heart rate slowed with it. I sat down on a cool metal bench for as long as I dared before heading back to the hospital.

I have to admit, I was not as in control of my feelings and emotions as I had thought I was. *Note to self: work on that!*

I wasn't hungry, but I stopped by the hospital cafeteria to buy a sandwich and another cup of coffee before going back to Mom's room.

I picked the table Mama Grace and I had sat at during breakfast and stared out at the wheat and cornfields.

After about half an hour, I felt a hand on my shoulder.

"How are you, Max?"

The face was familiar, but it took a few seconds for me to recognize it.

"Johnny … John Cottenfeld. How are you?" I answered.

"Max, I don't go by John or Johnny any more. It's *Jonathan* now." He pulled out a chair opposite me and sat even though I hadn't offered.

He sat there in his suit and tie, briefcase in hand. *I wonder what he thinks of my Harley shirt and leather jacket.*

Trying not to let my inner smirk show, I said, "Well, I stand corrected. Okay, then Jonathan it is. I still remember all the teasing you took about the name John. John this and John that, all referencing how you must have been named after a toilet. We were pretty cruel in those days."

"Yes, but no one does that anymore. I'm an attorney now and have one of the largest practices in Carbon. Respect is what I get today."

"Well congratulations John … I mean *Jonathan*." I couldn't help myself after the bragging he had just done.

"I came to the hospital today in hopes of seeing you, Max. As you may or may not know, your mother hired me as her attorney. I have been working with your mother and cousin Claudia to prepare for this day," he said.

I kept a flat expression and said nothing. He went on after an awkward pause. "I might as well be candid with you. Claudia shared that you have asked that all life support be removed. Probably a very wise decision if I do say so. From what Claudia said, your mother has only a few days left. Please accept my deepest sympathy."

"Oh, you're doing a bang-up job of expressing that, Johnny," I answered.

He went right on as if he had not heard me. "Now, in support of your mother's final wishes, Claudia has been given power of attorney and will act as executor of your mother's will. I will serve as the attorney of record. In fact, Claudia has been acting on your mother's behalf for some time and doing quite a nice job I might add. Your mother is lucky to have had her."

"I'm aware of all that. Claudia has told me as much," I responded.

"Good … Your mother does have a will. She has asked that immediately after the funeral all of those listed in it be present for a reading. That will take place in my office an hour or so after the funeral. Max, you are mentioned in the will, so you will need to attend."

"Well, that's a surprise! Me mentioned in her will? That must be a mistake."

"No, Max. It is real. You will need to attend."

"It should be worth it, Johnathan. I'm sure she will have left me a long letter on legal paper chewing my ass. I wouldn't miss it."

"Max, that's all I had to say. Again, my deepest sympathy." He stood and offered his hand.

"Thank you, John. Always good to visit with an old classmate," I said.

He turned and left the cafeteria without uttering another word.

Now I remember why we all thought he was an asshole in high school; he is an asshole!

* * *

Back in Mom's room and having assumed my position in my now favorite chair, I reflected on my talk with Jonathan Cottenfeld, Esquire. I still found it hard to believe that I was mentioned in her will. It had to be some kind of gag. *After taking a stand in high school about not wanting their money and having rejected their aid in everything in my life, why would she include me in her will? It's gotta be one final letter, a final chewing of my ass, one last attempt to put me in my place.*

You better believe I'll attend, Mom. I can't pass up knowing if you'll try to reach out from the grave and kick my ass one more time. It'll be that much richer if Mr. Esquire is the one to deliver the message.

That event was still a few days off. I looked at Mom and suddenly felt exhausted. All the caffeine in the world couldn't keep me awake.

heard something drop on the chair near me and opened my eyes. My watch said it was 4:58 p.m. *Claudia.*

"Hi, Max. How is our favorite patient?" Claudia asked as she walked to the bed to stroke Mom's hair.

"No change, Claudia," I flatly replied.

Claudia fawned over Mom and occasionally asked rhetorical questions.

She continued to coo over my mother and stroke her hair.

As if trying to break the strained air between us, I said, "Claudia, I had a chat with Jonathan Cottenfeld, Esquire, this afternoon."

Her head snapped around. Her eyes flashed. "What did Mr. Cottenfeld have to say?"

"For one thing, he was very complimentary of the job you've been doing for Mom," I said.

That seemed to put her at ease. She smiled. "What else did he say?"

"We talked through Mom's wishes. He explained that he is the attorney of record and that you will serve as executor for the will and estate."

"I had told you all of that, Max." She sounded defensive.

"Yes, Claudia. No surprises there. However, John did add that there will be a reading of Mom's will right after the funeral in his office. He said that all those listed in her will are to attend. And—surprise, surprise—he said that I *am* listed."

She turned and took a step toward me. The color rushed out of her face.

Half whispering, Claudia said, "Max, you told your parents that you wanted nothing to do with their money. You even told me that they had written you out of their wills years ago. There must be a mistake! Jonathan, I mean Mr. Cottenfeld, must be in error."

She looked apoplectic and sat down, barely taking time to move her purse.

"You're right. I did say those things, and I meant them then, and I mean them today. But make no mistake, old Mr. Esquire did say that I am mentioned in the will. We'll just have to see what it all means in a few days."

I was content to let it hang in the air like that, but Claudia was not.

She continued louder and leaning more toward Mother than toward me said, "Max, you have always known that I was to be the executor. You know your Mom and I have been close for years. I've spent untold hours running errands for her, taking her places and taking care of her ... This has to be a mistake."

I was enjoying the moment far too much. I sat still and relaxed, holding what I hoped to be an inscrutable expression and letting the empty spaces stay that way.

"Claudia, let's not get all worked up about this. We'll know what Mom had in mind in a few short days."

"It's just not fair, Max. It's just not fair."

Claudia carried on for a while, getting up, sitting back down, getting up again. Finally, after she had calmed down, I stood and put on my jacket. Claudia settled back into her chair and pulled it close to the bed.

What a day. I don't know what to feel.

As I left the room, I stopped at the foot of the bed and reached out for Mom's foot again. Silently I said, "Mom, it's okay to go now. It's okay."

Chapter 15

"Now this is a homecoming!" I said as I stepped into X Marks the Spot and saw several of my old buddies sitting at two tables that had been pushed together near the wall opposite the pool tables and close enough to the bar to give one a sense that the beer would flow freely and service be prompt.

Terry, Jim, and Herb. Three friends. Four beers.

I peeled off my jacket and tossed it over the back of an extra chair and grabbed my beer before even sitting down.

"How the hell have you been, Max?" Jim asked.

"Good, man! You?" I asked. "Shit. When was the last time I saw you?"

"Biloxi. Had to have been. Damn … long time. Never mind how long," he said.

That got a laugh, and Terry looked particularly pleased.

I guess after the conversation at breakfast, he thought I might need to see a few more friendly faces here in old Carbon.

I reached across the table. "Herb." He shook my hand and with his other slapped me on the shoulder. "Good to see you, my friend," I said.

"Glad to be here, Max. Terry caught me just as I was about to leave the house. I heard the phone and went back in to answer. Glad I did, man," he said.

"Thanks, Terry. You're the best," I said. I gave him a thump on the back and sat back down.

"Wow. It really has been a long time. The last time we were all in the same room was probably high school, and the last time me, Max, and Jim were together was in LA, I think," Herb said.

"Yeah, right before the two of you abandoned my ass and came back to Carbon," I said. "But I moved in with those two Marines who got me hooked on Harleys, so I owe ya one."

"Then Jim joined the Air Force and abandoned me," Herb said, elbowing Jim who'd just lifted his beer for a drink.

"What can I say, man. I couldn't stay away from Max," Jim said, averting a spilled beer crisis by deftly countering the slosh.

"Wait. What? You lost me," Terry said.

"When I moved to LA to attend college number four or something, I looked up Jim and Herb because I knew they'd moved there. We lived together for a while before they decided to move back to Carbon. Then after I joined the Air Force, Jim and I ran into each other down in Biloxi when he was also assigned there," I said.

"Small world. Real small," Terry said.

"So, what have we got here? Terry. Marines, right?" Herb said.

"Yes, sir. Semper fi!" Terry said.

"And two Air Force," Jim said indicating himself and me with a head bob.

"And one Army grunt," Herb said, tapping his chest with his nearly empty beer mug. "So, boys, did you ever run into each other over in Nam?"

"Nope, not me, but I hadn't been over there very long when that 135-millimeter rocket ran into me," said Terry, instinctively reaching for his cane. "Khe Sanh 1968. Marines sent me home to rehab for a year but with a leg full of shrapnel, they had to cut me loose."

Diana came over with another round. "Having fun, guys?"

"Yes, ma'am," said Jim.

As she walked away, Terry smiled and said, "I can't complain. Got to come home to that and open this bar."

"Cheers," I said, and we all raised our glasses to Terry. But behind the smiles hung something heavy.

After a long drink, Herb said, "Yeah. We were all pretty lucky. I saw some nasty shit, man."

"Yeah. I don't think anyone can really get it unless they were there," I said. I knew that Terry wouldn't talk about his experience with Diana. She'd told me she thought he had PTSD but wouldn't discuss it with anyone except other military guys who'd seen combat. *Maybe Terry needs to get some of this stuff off his chest too.* "When I was in Dong Ha, we were close enough to the DMZ that the NVA could hit our base with artillery. The stuff they used was often leftover artillery from the Korean War. It wasn't uncommon for us to be walking around and find shrapnel with U.S. markings. The NVA was shooting at us with our own ammunition!

"Our retaliatory air support for Dong Ha had to be scrambled from DaNang about a hundred miles away, so they were about an hour away. The NVA knew that, so they would shoot at us for an hour and then crawl back in their caves and bunkers and wait for our jets to arrive. After a while, the jets would go bingo on fuel and have to return to DaNang. Then the NVA would come out and send rockets and artillery shells our way again." I paused to take a drink. Everyone was still engaged, so I went on.

"The longest string of rocket attacks that our crew experienced was sixteen days in a row. Someone would yell, 'BOHICA!' and we all knew what was coming … bend over, here it comes again. We didn't wear insignia—or much else for that matter—because we wanted to make it difficult for a sniper to identify targets. It was hotter than hell there. We were allowed to wear whatever we wanted, anything to keep us cool. Ya know, we lost that site to rocket attacks three times."

"I hear ya," Jim said. "I didn't see much combat, but one of my best friends and drinking buddies saved my life."

We all shifted in our chairs and leaned in. I suspected each of us had had that happen at least once.

"Oh, yeah?" Terry encouraged Jim to go on.

"Yeah. So, one of my best friends and drinking buddies was a dude named Sergeant Mike Bass. We called him Fish—"

"Lemme guess," Herb said. "'Cuz he drank a lot.'" The corners of his mouth turned up and he pushed his beer back and looked back at Jim.

"Hey, who's telling this story?" Jim said, obviously amused. "*Yes.* Because he drank a lot."

"But a rocket attack one night sobered him right up. We were hanging around the camp when things started to land. It was a mad life or death scramble to the bunker. I fell just as I tried to duck inside. Fish grabbed me and threw me in, then jumped in himself. Just as he got in, a rocket hit and took the door of the bunker off."

Jim finished his story, then looked around. No one jumped in, so I did.

"My first night at Dong Ha was crazy. There was this steel revetment wall surrounding the site. It was twelve feet high and had two rows of steel separated by a four-foot void between the steel sections that had been filled with dirt all the way up. Twelve feet! A rocket had hit earlier and ripped up that wall. What was left of a radar van was there; it looked like the antenna dish had taken a direct hit. Most of the van had burned and was a molten mess. We met the crew we were replacing. They all looked shell shocked. One of the guys was in such bad shape he couldn't talk. He just sat in a corner, his body shaking uncontrollably.

"'Shit,' I thought. 'This is going to be my home for the rest of my tour. Shit! Shit! Shit!'

"I had hardly gotten that thought out of my head when another rocket attack started. I'd been in 75-millimeter mortar attacks before, but that was my first rocket attack. 135s were a whole different thing! They called it Boom Boom Junction for a reason.

"We sat in that bunker for what seemed like hours but was actually minutes. Some of the fellas that had been there for a while sat back and smoked cigarettes. I would hear the whoosh of a rocket and then an explosion and duck with every whoosh I heard. Finally, an old troop leaned over to me and said, 'Kid, you don't need to duck if you hear the whoosh. The whoosh means it's gone over you. It's when you don't hear the whoosh that your ass is grass.'"

Terry laughed and shook his head. "That's right," he said, slamming his beer mug down on the table. With that, he stood, up, grabbed his cane, and said, "I'm going to hit the head. Carry on."

"I'll go grab us another round," Herb said.

Jim slid his chair back too and said, "I'll be right back, Max. I want to go make a quick check-in call to my wife. She was pretty sick when I headed over here. I want to make sure she's okay. Be right back."

I was left alone with my memories of Dong Ha.

* * *

The smell of something resembling rotting fruit and fecal matter hit as soon as I stepped, healthy and whole, out of the bunker. I walked past the morgue tent stacked with the bodies of the men who'd never heard the whooshes. Just 60 feet separated the tent and bunk where I slept and the tent and tables where all those dead men lay. The identified remains were tagged, bagged, and secured in one tent, but the unidentified remained untagged and unbagged, rotting in the hot open air until properly identified.

My stomach clenched at the memory. I tried to wash the bile down with the last swig of beer in my mug, but its hoppy smell and warm slide down my throat only intensified things.

* * *

A thump on my left shoulder told me Terry had returned. Herb followed, four beers in hand. *Not bad. He looks like he could work here.*

Jim was right behind them.

"Lilly okay?" I asked as Jim returned and pulled out his chair.

"Oh, yeah. She's fine. Just a little under the weather, so I wanted to check in on her," said Jim.

"You treat that woman like a princess," Herb said. His eyes twinkled impishly but couldn't hide his genuine admiration.

"What can I say? I got me a good one. Right, Terry?"

"Right, man. Gotta take care of a good woman!" Terry replied.

Jim sat down, dragged the old wooden chair closer to the table, and said, "So Max, what's your story woman-wise? You and Jane still together?"

"No, man," I paused and took a drink. *Maybe fresh beer will settle my stomach and get me through this.*

Terry knew the story, but the other two raised their eyebrows and kept drinking without looking away, my sign that I was expected to bear my soul. *Jesus, guys get just as sappy as girls.*

"Nothing much to tell, really. She was a nice girl, but it just got weird. I'm remarried now. Much better situation," I continued.

"Weren't you two, you and Jane, I mean, engaged while you were overseas?"

"Yeah. That's part of why I didn't re-up. That and after basic, tech, and all the stuff I worked on while I was in the Air Force, I decided I wanted to go back to college for real. I had the GI Bill. Jane and I had met when I was stationed in Idaho. I'd be going back there, and it was close to The College of Idaho."

"Your mom was not happy, man. Not happy at all," Herb said. "I remember my mom asking me about you after she saw your mom in the grocery store one day. She was pissed you didn't stick around, and it sounds like engineer wasn't as impressive as doctor. Glad my parents never put that kind of pressure on me," he continued.

"Yeah, well. I think it's well established that Mom and Ed weren't exactly the nurturing types," I said. "In fact, hah, Jim, you probably remember this ... Wait, let me back up." I paused, took a drink, and started at the beginning.

"Before heading to basic in Texas, I was here in Carbon marking time. One day my mom says to me, 'Max, you say they will be sending you to technical school after basic training, but you have no idea where that will be. No telling where your final duty station will be. You may even be in Europe or some other remote place. Why don't you sign over the VW and the motorcycle to me? I'll make sure they're stored until you want them. Then Ed and I can get them to you when you're settled. You should also sign over your checking account until you get somewhere permanent. You never know how well you will be able to take care of your money in a barracks with a bunch of people you don't know—"

"Yep. I remember," Jim said, shaking his head.

"So, Jim shows up at Biloxi about two months into my training, and we go for a beer to catch up. A few days later, he comes up to me in the barracks holding a copy of Carbon's newspaper that his mother had sent him. He says to me, 'Hey, Max. I didn't know your car was for sale. Wish I would have known that, I would have liked to get a good used VW.' 'What the hell are you talking about?'" I asked him.

"He showed me the paper and, sure enough, there was the ad. The number to call for information was my folks' home number."

Jim jumped in. "You should have seen him. He about blew a gasket."

"It wasn't pretty," I admitted. "I called them that night after my shift. My mom told me that they'd sold both the VW and the motorcycle *and* closed my checking account!" I could feel the heat rising from my chest to the crown of my head as if it was happening all over again.

I got more animated. "'What do you think you're doing?' I asked her. 'You have no right to do that shit.'" Shifting into my mother's voice, I haughtily continued. "'Now Max, do not use that kind of language on your mother. Remember, you must respect and love your mother.'"

"Seriously, man?" Herb asked.

"Oh yeah. That's one hundred percent pure Pearl Ellis right there, my friend," I replied.

I went on with the story. "'Respect and love, my ass!' I told her. 'Those were my things. What gave you the right?' Then I asked her where the money was and told her I wanted it. She told me all the money had gone toward my expenses. Expenses. What a woman!" I picked the beer up and set it back down without taking a sip.

"She said that she and Ed had incurred a lot of *expenses* for me over the years: braces in eighth grade, two grand; books, clothes, and school supplies; and, of course, the dry-cleaning bills after I left, for what I have no idea. Oh yeah, and the damage that had happened to the Chevy when I was in that accident. She let me know that when all of my expenses were added up, 'They were a tidy sum!' she said. And the money they'd taken from my account and from selling my motorcycle and the VW didn't cover it all."

"That sucks, Max," Terry said, patting me on the back.

I suppressed my rage. "What are ya gonna do, right?" I responded with a shrug. "I was broke but not broken." I looked at each of the men at the table. "We've all been there. We saw hell overseas, and here we are. That which doesn't kill us makes us stronger, right guys?" I said, lifting a beer in salute.

"Amen, brother," Herb said as we clanked glasses and downed whatever beer was left in them.

Jim was the one to say what was on all our faces. "Well, boys, it's been fun. But this old man needs to hit the hay."

"Yeah. I'd better get some beauty sleep. Thanks for arranging this, Terry. This has been great. I'll try to catch up with you guys again before I leave," I said as we all stood and gathered our things.

Before he left, I yelled after Jim, "Hey, I hope Lilly gets to feeling better soon!"

He turned and said, "Thanks, Max. Next time you're in town, let's get together with the wives."

"Sounds great, Jim. You'll love Beth."

He waved and gave a thumbs up.

Chapter 16

Seeing the guys had been great, but my body felt heavy. I was tired but couldn't rest. My mind jumped from memory to memory.

* * *

"Jane, stay for a while," I said into her neck. Her hair smelled like strawberries, and her skin was smooth as I moved my palms up and down her arms.

She pressed into me, and I pushed the fabric of her shirt up her back until it untucked from her skirt and exposed the skin of her back and belly.

We kissed and wrapped our bodies around each other. I wanted to stop her, stop myself. But this time, I didn't.

Immediately following the encounter, I was sick about what we had done. With Jane's body in my arms, all the sexual things from my childhood ran through my head. I blamed myself. *How could I have done this?* I could hear my mom's voice yelling at me for not being clean anymore. Worse, thoughts of being the man of the house flashed through my mind. Every sexual innuendo my mom had ever used flooded my brain.

What if Jane gets pregnant?

Jane's body relaxed, and her breathing became rhythmic. But the longer we lay there the more tense my body got and the more my mind raced. *Jesus, I am fucked!*

"Jane, I need to get you home. Wake up," I said, trying not to shake her too hard.

After delivering Jane back to her dorm that night, I sat in the dark in my apartment. The shame was overwhelming. I did not sleep at all that night.

You cannot tell anyone what you did. Not because it was dirty—God, you did enjoy it—but because you can't admit that to anyone. She didn't do anything wrong either; she was wonderful. No. You just can't let this get out. Oh my God, what am I going to do? I can't react the same way I did with those other girls when I got close to going too far. I can't dump Jane and run. She might dump me, but I will not dump her.

* * *

"Hi, Jane. Sorry I haven't been able to see you for the past week. I've been really busy with work," I said, shifting the receiver from one hand and ear to the other.

"Hi, Max. That's okay. It's been a busy week for me too. What are you doing tonight?" she asked from the other end of the line. Her voice reflected her usual jovial self. *She's fine while I'm a wreck. I like this girl, but what have I done? I'm not ready to get married. Geez, Max, guess you should've thought about that before you slept with her. You've got to do your duty now.*

"That's what I was calling to ask you. Would you like to go to dinner?" I asked.

* * *

I pulled the sheets around me and rolled over in my borrowed bed. *Dinner and a marriage proposal and I'd sealed my fate.* I stared at the shadows on the wall opposite the bed.

* * *

"Max, it's so nice to have you back from Vietnam. Jane hasn't been able to stop talking about you since you left. It's good to see you two finally hitched," one of Jane's uncles said as he passed another wedding gift toward Jane and me.

Mom piped up and fifteen or so faces turned toward her. "Max, now let me ask you something. Now that you are married, you are *clean* for your wedding night, aren't you?"

All conversation stopped. Everyone in the room looked at Mom like she had just farted. Jane and I looked at each other, embarrassed.

Mom sat there cool as ever. I wanted to hit her and wipe that fucking smirk off her face.

"Mom, that is none of your goddamned business. Now shut your damned mouth and let us open these gifts."

She snapped her head from me to the room and flashed an awful smile. "Isn't he the sweetest boy to joke with his mother that way?" she asked with a giggle. No one else in the room smiled.

"Shut up, Mom. Or get your ass out of here now."

* * *

Clean. I'd always known Mom was full of it, but if only I'd remained "clean" then I wouldn't have ended up marrying someone out of guilt. Guilt and duty aren't good ingredients for a happy relationship.

I rolled over again and closed my eyes. In my mind's eye, I saw myself pulling one of the familiar 8½ × 4-inch, orange envelopes with extra postage to cover its heft from the cubby slot marked with my name. I didn't need to look at the return address to know that it was from Mrs. E. Ellis of West 9th St. Carbon, Kansas.

* * *

At 5:02 p.m., I headed to my car. Sitting in the front seat, I opened the envelope and pulled out what without counting felt like at least twelve pages of vitriol typed using the legal-sized carriage of Ed's office typewriting.

Hello, Max.

Your first reaction will likely be one of surprise that I address you at the office. But read on. As an interested party, I need to talk alone with you and, while there, it was apparent the opportunity would not arise, so I took your office address from the phone book.

Max, I'm going to try to talk with you—NOT as your mother—but as a cherished acquaintance who is vitally concerned in whatever befalls you. But I cannot refrain from remembering those years gone by when you and I were not only related but were the best of warm friends who shared moments of effort, faith, thought dreams, and good or bad reality.

...I've been doing much research on some of your challenges and had hoped to Xerox full pages from references books I found at the city and college libraries, but it wouldn't work ... I must clearly and bluntly point out... I'm of the opinion that ... Daddy and I have talked at length about you and your work ...

The Reader's Digest, *August issue, said, "Most of us live our lives the way we watch TV. Even though the program isn't as good as we would like it to be, we are too lazy to get up and change it."*

Let's talk over some ideas—eh?

And on and on ... *Our love and STAND TALL,*

Mama and Daddy

* * *

Love and stand tall, my ass. Those letters were full of hate and meant only to tear me down—me and Jane down.

I sat up in bed and gave the pillow a few thumps with my fists. *Joke's on you, Mom. Your letters really pissed us off at first but then we just saw them and you as a joke—a big, miserable joke.*

Not that she was right or that that letter had anything to do with marriage, but my mind wandered to years later when, pushing forty, I decided it was time to find myself and make some meaningful corrections. Sixty-five-year-old, seen-it-all counselor Irene Wilson was a perfect pick.

"Alright, Max. You know I care about you, but you're beating around the bush here. Just come right out and say what you need to say. This is a safe space," she said one day.

"What do you want me to tell you, Irene?" I snapped back.

She just sat there and let the silence stand.

"Do you want me to tell you about how my mom used to walk around without any clothes on, make me kiss her on the lips, and that she grabbed and touched me in ways that would turn your skin cold?"

I waited for her to laugh me off. She didn't. She just sat there with a blank look.

"Do you want me to tell you about Jane and the fact that I asked her to marry me out of feelings of guilt over having had sex prior to marriage? Do you want me to tell you about the rage I feel when I read stories in the paper about child abuse or see a show on TV about incest or some other form of abuse? Because I don't think I can."

Irene's face softened. She leaned toward me and waited for me to make eye contact.

"Max, I think that as a result of your childhood you

learned to suppress your feelings, except anger. It's a skill you've refined as you've gotten older. Your experiences in Vietnam probably only made it worse. Your biggest challenges in life will be to let yourself *feel* something other than guilt and rage. Max, I don't think you know how to feel or know what true feelings are."

I sat back in the chair. She was right.

* * *

After a while, I did let go of anger and guilt in some areas. Jane and I divorced, and I moved on. But regardless of my desire to get over my hate, I couldn't free myself of it. Even now when my mother could do nothing to hurt me, I despised her. For someone who wasn't good at feeling, I always did a bang-up job with that one.

As I dropped my head back onto the pillow another thick orange envelope came to mind and the events that had preceded it. For a moment I wished I'd had more to drink that night. Maybe I'd have been able to sleep.

* * *

"Max, you must come home," Mom said from over a thousand miles away.

"Mom, you can call as many times as you want, but the answer will always be the same. *No.* I am not coming back. I see no need."

"Max, your grandmother is dying. And she is so disappointed that you haven't come to see her."

"Mom, I highly doubt that. You've said yourself that she can't even remember who you are most days and that she's not in her right mind."

"Well, Max, that may be true, but nearly every time I see her, she asks about you. And when I tell her you're too busy, she tells me what a disappointment you've been to her. She's always loved you so much, Max. But you just don't seem to have any feelings at all. I can't say I disagree with Mother's disappointment right now, but I remain hopeful that your sense of familial duty will rise and that you'll find it within yourself to do what's right."

"And," she continued, "when the time comes, I hope you'll love your mother and do your duty."

Love your mother. Do your duty. What does she know about love or duty?

"Mom, you're not dying. I'm not going to talk about this with you right now. Besides, I've told you. After Vietnam I've had a hard time with death and funerals. You know this."

"Oh, Max. Don't be silly. This is different. It's completely different."

"It's not, Mom. But even if it was, why can't you just respect my position?"

"Come now, Max—"

"Goodbye, Mother," I said and hung up the phone.

A few weeks later, the phone rang again.

"Oh, Max. Ma Bess is gone. I did what I could, but she's gone." Mother sounded genuinely upset but who could know.

"Max, will you come home now? Come for the funeral."

"Mom, I'm not coming."

"Well then. I cannot for the life of me figure out why. Your grandmother loved you, and you say you loved your grandmother, but—"

"Mom, please. I can't. I just can't. You know why."

"Fine, Max. We'll send you pictures."

I could barely contain my rage and push down the images in my mind. "Mom, *please*. I've seen my share of death. I don't need pictures of my dead grandmother."

I hung up before she could argue and sunk into a chair in the living room. Choking back tears, I remembered all the good times I'd had with Ma Bess—playing ball in the back yard, her terrible cooking but delicious desserts, the way she looked at Mom and looked at me as if she somehow understood maybe not why but that there was some gulf between us and that she was on my side. *I wonder if Ma Bess saw Mom's over-the-top, you must love your mother obsession the way I do. Maybe that's why she kept her distance and guarded her independence.*

Mom's going to make a spectacle at the funeral, and I want to always remember Ma the way I do now—in her prime. I'm going to remember her in the good times. I know how my grandmother really felt about me, and I'm not going to let Mom alter the facts. I loved my grandmother.

Ten days after Ma Bess' funeral, a thick envelope arrived in the mail. In it were many photos. The top one was of Ma Bess in her casket.

Mom. You bitch!

I didn't need to look to know what the rest showed.

Cold sweat broke the surface of my skin, and I tossed the sheets aside and sat on the edge of the bed. I couldn't push down the memories I'd remembered back then.

* * *

"Alright, men. Here we are. Phu Bai. You know what to do. Up and operational!" With that, the commander turned and walked away. As we'd arrived, my buddy Bronc had said, "There it is," which was shorthand for "They fucked us again."

And fucked us they had. We were out on the perimeter of the base. Not another thing around, just open space. Whoever had picked this site placed it right in the middle of a Vietnamese graveyard. Not beside the graveyard, right in the middle of it.

Who is the dumb son of a bitch that picks these sites? I've got only forty-five days left on this tour. Why does it have to be hell all the way until wheels up?

The heat was stifling and sweat was already dripping down the sides of my body when I picked up a shovel. Fifty graves. Fifty bodies. Fifty faces. I'd been trying to shake those images for years. Mom had a television like everyone else while I was in Vietnam. She had to have had some idea of what it was like for me. *She just doesn't give a shit,* I'd thought as I dumped the face-down pictures in the trash.

* * *

I longed for sleep, but my thoughts and emotions rose and fell like waves, and images and smells of naked bodies alive and dead flooded me.

Part III: Gone, not Gone

Chapter 17

"Max ... Max, wake up," It was Diana.

"What time is it?" I asked, confused.

"It's just a bit past four, Max."

I knew what that meant.

"Max, the hospital called. Your mom passed away fifteen minutes ago." Diana said.

As I got dressed to go to the hospital all I could feel was the finality of it all. Was it really going to be over?

* * *

Claudia was standing outside Mom's room when I arrived.

"Oh Max, she's gone," she said, sobbing. "I loved her so much, and now she's gone."

"Claudia, this is not a surprise. We knew the end was coming—and soon. Let's look at it like she's in a better place now," I said.

"You're right. We have to move on now." With that, all the sobbing was gone. I instinctively raised an eyebrow and pulled a face. Claudia had always been something of a drama queen.

The bed in Mom's room was empty. She had been placed on a gurney. A sheet completely covered her body. The room had already been cleaned. The bed had been made. The flowers were gone from the windowsill, and all other papers and cards were gone. The room looked like it was ready for the next patient.

I stepped back into the hallway. This was different from the dead bodies I had been around in Vietnam, and I had wanted her gone. Still, I was not comfortable in that room with her body.

Claudia was back in the hallway too. Her tears were all gone as she began to get to the business at hand.

"Max, we have a lot to do today," she began. "I want you to come to the house with me. We need to pick out clothes for your mother to be buried in, we need to write an obituary, and we need to get with the funeral home to make all of the final arrangements. You know that as executor, I have a number of duties. Many of those duties will be dealing with your mom's property and finances. I just want you to know that I will see that you are treated fairly. Trust me on that."

I knew a line of bullshit when I heard it. *Trust me. Right!*

"Whoa, Claudia. You told me Mom did not want me in her house. And you're her executor. Aren't you the one who has the final say on arrangements? You don't need me."

"Max, forget about what your mom said about the house. I'm in charge now, so we will do it my way. And I do need your help. I know your mother's wishes, but I will make adjustments when I think they're necessary."

I smiled. *This is going to be interesting. Claudia is large and in charge and liking this.*

She continued, "I am the executor. However, I will want your input on some things as we go forward. I need to run to the bank. Listen, why don't we meet at her house at eleven. I will go pick Joe up, and we'll meet you there. There are just so many things to do, Max. I have to make this a wonderful funeral for your mom, one that will make the people in this town stand up and take notice."

With that she turned and was off.

* * *

It was just before 5:00 a.m. at home when Beth answered.

"Max, is that you?" she asked without waiting for my greeting.

"Yes, babe. Wanted to call and let you know that it's all over. Mom died about two hours ago."

"How are you doing, sweetheart?"

"You know, I think I'm fine. I'm reminded of Martin Luther King Junior when he said, 'Free at last, free at last, thank God Almighty I'm free at last.' I think I'm okay."

"Are you staying for the funeral?"

"Yes. I imagine the funeral will be in two or three days. I'll head home after that."

Just hearing Beth's voice made me relax. I would be okay.

I walked back by Mom's room on the way out of the hospital. The gurney was gone.

Hang in there, buddy. Just a few more days and this bullshit will all be over. No more hatred. It will be over when the dirt hits that casket.

* * *

It seemed strange to ride the hog up the street and into the driveway of Mom's house. She would go ballistic if she could see this. *What will the neighbors think—a motorcycle! A derelict dressed in leathers too! What is the Ellis household coming to?*

The thought of that scene made me smile. What was funnier was to think that my mother ever thought her neighbors thought of her as on par with them.

At least the house was still standing. That was noteworthy.

* * *

"I'm not going to pay some greedy contractor to build our house," Ed said to my mother as he erased a line on what must've been the seventh draft of the plans and drew in a wall somewhere else. The drawings looked more like a plan for a mouse maze than a home people could live in.

"Well, you can't build it yourself, Ed," Mom said while motioning for him to push out a kitchen wall.

"I've got it covered, Pearlie. I went down to the high school today and talked to several of the maintenance guys there. I'm going to hire them to build it for us."

* * *

As I walked up to the front door that was like the other front door but on the side of the house opposite the oddly pushed out family room, the perennially problematic lawn lay to my left.

* * *

"Ed, the zoysia isn't taking. It's been weeks, and all we've got is a lawn full of brown grass plugs. It's embarrassing. We don't need golf course grass anyway. We need a good quality seed and some high-quality fertilizer."

I leaned in. Something told me this was going to be rich!

"And where are you going to get high-quality shit, Pearl?" Ed said everything like he was delivering lines to an adoring audience. "And how much will this golden MiracleGrow cost me?"

"Ed!"

"I'm going to get it from the city wastewater plant, and it won't cost a dime," she said.

* * *

Memories of Mom and I hauling bushel baskets of shit in the old 1951 Chevy were just the mood booster I needed before stepping into that house. I could almost still smell the soggy sludge and see the hundreds of tomato plants that inexplicably sprouted throughout the yard. *Mom, I wonder if every time the neighbors flush their toilets, they think of highfalutin Pearlie Ellis.*

Claudia opened the door as I walked up.

"Great, you are right on time. Come in. We need to get to work."

Still laughing inside and wondering what fresh hell awaited, I forgot to step over the not-quite-right threshold and tripped going into the foyer. *Well, Mom. At least you built on the right side of town, huh?*

Claudia's husband, Joe, stood nearby. We greeted one another and moved toward the kitchen where Claudia was to hold court.

The house was so hot and stuffy I half expected to find Ed watching football in his den, one of the only rooms he'd been willing to pay to have air-conditioned. *I wonder how much those cheapskates would've have charged me if my room had been air-conditioned.*

Walking down the hall, there it was on the left.

"Max! Don't open that." Claudia furrowed her brows and did everything but purse her lips. "You know you're not supposed to be in there."

"Seriously, Claudia? She is gone. I just want to see it. What's the harm?"

"Well, don't go in," she responded.

No Ed, but the room looked just the way he must've left it on the day he died. His magazines were there caked in a layer of dusty film, cigar, ashtray. The recreation room was the same way.

Chapter 18

"Now, here are the chores we need to do immediately." Claudia started in before any of us even sat down. "Joe and I stopped by the bank, Max. Everything is set there. I have been on your Mom's checking and savings account for years and as such can write checks and withdraw money as needed. So, I will be in charge of all things having to do with money, which will be almost everything."

"As I see it," she continued, "Max, you should write the obituary. After all, she was your mother, and you probably know more of the details of her early life. Joe and I will review and approve it when you have it completed. Joe and I will go through the house and make sure everything is in order. I will also pick out her clothing for the funeral home."

She was on a roll. "This afternoon we will all go to the funeral home to pick out a casket and make final arrangements."

"Ok? Let's get moving." She motioned at me. "You can sit here at the kitchen table while Joe and I start through the house to make sure everything's in order."

Uh huh. Going through the house to make sure everything's in order my ass. A quick inventory of the items you and Joe are going to get is what you really mean. You should have been Mom's daughter. The two of you have so many things in common.

While Claudia and Joe were in the garage, I snuck to the back of the house. It was obvious that long ago, most likely the day he died, Mom had moved out of their bed and into my old room. *In remembrance of Ed, I'm sure!* Seeing what I didn't need to see, I went back to the kitchen and tried to focus on writing my mom's obituary.

I sat there for several minutes listening to furniture and boxes being slid across floors, the opening and closing of doors, and muffled conversation.

It took about an hour, but I wrote the obituary. I tried to do a good job of writing about the positive things in her life: childhood on the farm, her Miss Bradley title, college in Wichita, and so on. When it came to the survived-by portion, I included myself, Claudia, and Joe. I also included Beth and all four of our children: Nick, Anne, and Beth's oldest two boys.

"Okay, Claudia." I called down the hall from the doorway of the kitchen. "I finished my homework. Come take a look."

"Max, we can't have your marriage to Beth mentioned, and no children other than Nick can be listed."

"What!" I demanded. "What do you mean *can't have?*"

"Your mother never recognized your marriage to Beth after you divorced Jane, and she certainly did not count those children as her grandchildren."

"Claudia that is bullshit! I frankly do not care what Mom thought. She is dead and gone. This obituary is for the living to read. This obit will be published as written with Beth and the kids listed, or I'm out of here now. Either go along with me on this or stuff this whole funeral up your ass, and I'll just leave it all to you. Your choice, Ms. Executor!"

"Now wait a minute, you two," Joe jumped in. "Claudia, Max has a point. Let's do it his way and try to get through these next few days amicably."

After some thought, she said, "Okay, Joe. But I am not used to not getting my way. I don't like it. I'm not happy!"

"Tough shit, Claudia. Thanks Joe," I responded.

* * *

"Claudia, you ordered enough flowers to fill a basketball court," I said as we stepped out of the flower shop. "Is this really necessary?"

"Yes, Max. It is necessary. I want to give your mother a proper funeral. And now that I know what flowers will be on her casket, we can go to the funeral home.

"I have to say, I'm really surprised that Mom requested that her funeral be held at the funeral home rather than her church," I said.

"The minister from her church will officiate. She probably felt it would be easier for everyone not to have to be moving back and forth between the funeral home, the church, and the grave site."

I wasn't convinced.

* * *

As we were walking to the back area of the funeral home to view their selection of caskets, we passed a room that's door was partially open. I glanced in without thinking. A steel slab table was in view. Laying on the table was Mom. Completely naked. I snapped my head away as soon as I could, but it was as if she had reached out one more time and said, "Gotcha, son!"

"Max, I am so sorry!" said the funeral director reaching across me to grab the knob and pull the door shut. Too stunned to respond, I simply took another step down the hallway and tried to catch up with Claudia.

As he ushered us into the large room at the end of the hall, the director said, "I'll leave you two to look around and discuss things, but I'll be back in ten or fifteen minutes to check on you and answer any questions you have. Is that okay?"

"Yes, of course," Claudia responded immediately and as if she was the only one who'd been asked.

As the director turned to leave, Claudia turned her attention to the displays. I simply followed her around as she pretended to be interested in several of the caskets.

"I don't get it, Claudia," I said as my cousin ran her hands over the cream-colored satin lining of a large oak casket.

"Don't get what?" she asked.

"Why Mom wouldn't insist on a church service for her funeral."

Claudia gave me an exasperated look and said, "I don't know, Max. What's it matter to you?"

"Never mind! I was just trying to talk to you." I left her to her shopping and found an overstuffed recliner off to the side where I could sit with my thoughts.

* * *

When we moved to Carbon, the whole family became members of the First Methodist Church.

It was a beautiful church in the middle of downtown. It also had the largest membership, even more than St. Mary's Catholic Church.

During the first few years we were in Carbon, we went to church every Sunday as a family. I also attended Sunday school and a Monday night youth group. I enjoyed going because a lot of my classmates also attended.

Ed had been elected to one of the church governing committees too.

If it was Sunday morning, the Ellis family was at the First Methodist Church—or at least some of us were.

My mother quit going. She would say that she needed to stay home because she was busy with something or other. *You've got nothing but time now, Mom. So, what's your excuse not to be in church now?*

* * *

"I've made my selection. I'm going to go find Mr. Ashton. You just wait here while I talk to him about a few other details," Claudia said as she approached.

"Yes, ma'am," I replied and gave her a dismissive salute. "You know where to find me when you're done."

* * *

"Team tryouts start in a couple weeks," Ed said to my mother not me, but I chimed in anyway.

"I need to start practicing."

"That's a good idea," Mom said.

Ed ignored both comments. "The commissioner said he'd have the paperwork filed by the end of the week. It'll be ready in time."

Mother nodded like she understood, but I had no idea what he was talking about.

"Think Coach will let me on the team?" I asked my mother.

"Why don't you ask him?" she said, gesturing to Ed.

I furrowed my brows at Ed who chuckled. "I don't know, Max. We'll have to see your swing."

They both laughed. I only stared.

Mother caught my look. "We told you, didn't we? I'm sure we did. Ed's starting his own team. The Methodist Braves."

Methodist Braves?

"Why?"

"It'll improve my position in the community," Ed said, chewing his meatloaf as he talked. I looked away, disgusted. Also, disinterested. I couldn't wait for my team to pound the stupid Braves.

"As a sponsor, my name will be all over the place." Ed looked around the room and waved his fork at the walls. "I can see the signs now. My name will be on all the lists and beside all the big names on the advertising boards. Ed Ellis … Carbon's premier accountant!"

I was only half listening, more interested in finishing my meatloaf before him so I could have the last piece on the plate. It had a caramelized top that looked particularly tasty.

I perked up, though, when he said he wanted only the best players. He gestured to me when he said it.

I lowered my fork, a bite of meatloaf still on it.

"Huh?"

"Don't say *huh*," Mother corrected.

"I'm in seventh grade now. I'm trying out for the Comets."

"Don't be ridiculous, Max," Mother said. Ed dove into his meatloaf knowing, as I did, that my mother had just taken over the conversation. "Of course, you'll play for Ed's team."

"But … I worked so hard so I could play for the Comets." They knew this. They *knew* it. "Coach said I have a good chance."

"How would that look? Playing for another team. No, you'll play for Ed."

I stared at her, my bite of meatloaf still stuck on my fork. She cut her own meatloaf in that meticulous way of hers and took a bite. I could see I'd already lost the argument.

I looked at Ed. "Who's coaching? You?"

Ed had just swallowed his last bite of meatloaf. He guffawed. "Do you think I want to coach a bunch of rowdy brats? No thank you. That'll be Duane Riddle's job. I'm paying for things. That's the important part. Duane works for me; he'll do it."

He reached his fork across the table and speared the last coveted piece of meatloaf. He plopped it on his plate and began to eat without a thought.

* * *

"Max? I'm ready to go." Claudia was tucking paperwork into her oversized purse as she approached my chair.

"That was fast," I said.

"Well, I know what I—," she corrected herself, "what your mother liked."

I nodded and used getting up from the chair as a way to hide my smirk.

Claudia pointed to a large, well-crafted casket with a silver satin liner. "That's the one. What do you think?"

"It's very nice. Looks expensive," I said.

"It was. It was the most expensive one, but I'm not worried about that. I just want to honor your mother by giving her a proper funeral."

There probably won't even be fifty people in attendance. Who are you trying to impress?

As we stepped through the front doors and looked out on the parking lot, Claudia added, "I made arrangements for us to use the Cadillac limousine for the ride to cemetery too."

Mom is going out in style! Hang in there, Max. Only three days. Only three more days.

"Max, it's been a long day. Why don't you join Joe and me for a nice dinner? We can pick Joe up on our way."

I could see that Claudia and I were headed for a train wreck. I just wanted to get out of town without that happening. "No thanks, Claudia. It has been a long day. I'm going to head back to Terry and Diana's to rest. I'll see you at the funeral."

Chapter 19

Three days of pouring beer, shooting pool, and visiting with Diana and Terry was like being in heaven. Diana had always been the closest thing I had to a sister.

While setting up the bar for opening the day after Mom died, Diana said, "It's so good to have you here, Max. I wish Beth could've come too. We didn't really get a chance to get to know her when the two of you came last time."

"Beth is great, but Mom and Ed were never welcoming to her. Funny because Mom was always such a bitch to Jane and even did things to break up our marriage, but when we divorced, Mom suddenly took Jane under her wing and even stayed with her one time when she came up to see me and Nick."

"You two were married for a long time. If you don't mind me asking, what happened?" Diana wiped the outside of a glass, flipped it over, and set it on the drainage rack with about twelve others, and looked over at me.

"It was both our faults, I guess. Truthfully, I married her for the wrong reasons. And when she got sick—or claimed to be sick, no one could ever confirm any issues—things just deteriorated. I was doing everything—earning the money, taking care of Nick, taking care of the house. We weren't really in love, but it wasn't all bad either. I didn't want to leave, but I didn't want to stay. Eventually, I realized that things were as good as they would ever get, and that wasn't okay with me," I said.

"I'm sure it was harder because you two had a kid together."

"Yeah. That was part of it, but Nick and I were always close. A divorce wasn't going to change that, and Jane is a caring mom. When we first separated, Nick lived with her and we saw each other all the time. But just two months after the divorce, Jane got remarried. That was not a good situation. Nick moved in with me."

"Does Nick talk to her much?" Diana asked.

"Oh yeah. Jane took her parenting of Nick seriously and never missed an opportunity to spend time with him. She remains a big part of his life to this day."

"So, tell me about Beth. How'd you two meet?"

"After the divorce, I dated a number of women. I just wanted to find someone that I loved, that I respected, that I enjoyed being with and someone that shared the same goals and desires that I did." I couldn't believe I was telling her that. She was almost as easy to talk to as Beth.

I went on. "As long as both Nick and I were satisfied with frozen TV dinners, we were in good shape. I didn't cook, and I was not about to learn. We were getting along fine."

Diana laughed and took another glass from the dishwasher rack and began to buff off the water spots. "I know some guys like that."

I smiled and leaned against the bar. "About a year and a half after the divorce, a friend said she had found just the woman for me. She set up a blind date. From what I was told about this woman, I was anxious to meet her. We arranged a dinner date. I rang the bell and a cute thirteen-year-old opened the door. I introduced myself and asked if her mom was there. She looked me up and down, smiled, and turned around, 'Mom, he's here,' then she stuck her hand out and said, 'I'm Anne.' I knew from that moment that Anne and I were going to get along fine. Then around the corner came a beautiful blond."

"Sounds like you were smitten, my friend," Diana said.

"Absolutely. I knew that night was not going to be one I would soon forget. During dinner, I learned that Beth had three children. Beside Anne, she had two grown boys that had already left home and were on their own. She had been married once, for nineteen years, and had been divorced for about six. She had her own business, a beauty shop that she operated out of the basement of her home. She had been the primary breadwinner for her family for many years—even during her previous marriage. She was—and is—pretty funny. She told me that by getting a divorce, she had lost a dependent. We got along great. We shared work and divorce stories, talked politics and hobbies. It was a great night!"

I laughed.

"What's so funny?" Diana asked.

"When leaving the restaurant, Beth asked me to drive her by the engineering firm where I worked. When we arrived, she asked that I walk her around for a tour. As we were leaving, she apologized and said, 'I just wanted to make sure you have a job. I don't want to date another dependent.'"

"Very practical," Diana said with a laugh. "A match made in heaven."

"On our second date, we went to a movie—all three of us. I had Beth on one side of me and Anne on the other. Anne was full of questions. I think she was at first being protective of her mother, and second was sizing me up for herself. We all had a great time, and Anne and I bonded. Shortly thereafter, I introduced Nick to Beth and Anne. Nick was several years younger than Anne, but they hit it off. Nick fell for Beth immediately. In fact, Nick had some sage advice for me a couple of weeks after meeting her. 'Dad, don't screw this up. She's wonderful.'"

"She really does sound great, Max. So, when did you ask her to marry you?

"Not wanting to make another marriage mistake, I drug my feet. It took me over a year and a half to ask her. Thankfully, she said yes, and we got married precisely two years to the day from when we met. There's just no comparison between my life with Beth and my life with Jane. Beth accepts you for who you are, and as long as you're fair and stay the course, she's going to treat you well. She values other's opinions. That was something that Jane, and my mom for that matter, never did. Beth's idea of a marriage is that you're in it together and must remain committed for it to work. Beth isn't out to be taken care of. She is always pitching right there along with you, cheering you on. Her goal is never selfish, she wants her family to be successful and happy in their own rights."

"I'm so happy for you, Max. I hope that with your mother's passing, you can put all the bad stuff in the past." Diana patted my back and headed to unlock the bar door.

I hoped so too as I remembered receiving another one of Mom's nastygrams. She introduced herself to Beth with a rather lengthy legal-sized, type-written letter explaining all the things she had done for me over the years and what an ungrateful son I had been. "Oh, and by the way," she'd added, "welcome to the family."

Mom never made an effort to find anything out about Anne or Beth's older boys. In telephone conversations, she would only acknowledge Nick.

It was fine for divorced Ed to adopt me, but Mom couldn't find it within herself to adopt by acknowledgement her new step-grandchildren.

Chapter 20

I got up early on the day of the funeral and packed the hog being careful not to wrinkle the clothes I intended to wear at the funeral. It would be the funeral, the visit to the lawyer's office and then out on the road and headed for home. If all went well, I was sure to make it to Wichita by nightfall.

Diana, Terry, and I had said our goodbyes the night before. They would be at the funeral, but we might not get a chance to talk.

The county road was nearly deserted as I headed for town. Breakfast at Barry's sounded good. Then I'd go to the funeral home to change clothes and wait for the main event.

As I rode, the air seemed fresher. The colors from the early morning sun were brighter. And somehow, I felt more alive than I had in years. I would see dirt on the casket and know that she was gone. Then the healing would begin.

I was smiling as I parked in front of Barry's. I revved the engine just so I could hear the pipes. *God, I love that sound.*

There wasn't much of a crowd. A couple of booths were filled, and three old guys were sitting at the counter. Dressed in my motorcycle clothes, I got a few strange looks as I found a place at the counter.

Something greasy sounded good. So, it was hash browns, sausage, toast, and coffee for me.

As I sat there, I couldn't help but hear the three old guys as they drank their coffee and talked to the cashier.

I thought I recognized the loudest one of them as one of Ed's old clients. I thought he ran a lumber company and hardware store or something like that.

"Say, any of you guys going to Pearlie Ellis' funeral today?"

"Yeah, I am," the loud guy said.

He continued. "I went to the viewing last night. They made old Pearlie look pretty good. Claudia was there. She was all broken up. Crying her eyes out. Pearlie was lucky to have such a nice gal looking out for her."

I had skipped the viewing. I was glad I had missed the Claudia show too.

One of the other guys chimed in. "That Claudia is a peach, the way she looked after Pearlie after Ed died."

Now it was the third guy's turn. "Wasn't there a boy, a son, in the mix too? What ever happened to him?"

The loud guy answered. "He's a no-good son of a bitch. He shit all over his parents years ago, and they threw him out. You know Ed adopted that little bastard. He was Pearlie's from her first marriage. The shithead better not show up now; he would probably get the shit kicked out of him if he did."

They all had a good laugh over that threat.

Doesn't know his ass from third base.

Their words reminded me of the good Christian fella at the gas station when I was pulling into town. I smiled thinking maybe I should get out of town while the getting was good. I paid my tab. As I left, I thought about introducing myself and asking Mr. Loudmouth if he wanted to try to kick the shit out of me.

No, this is not going to be a day for making trouble. This is the day that will set me free. I just need to keep smiling and thinking about being free at last.

* * *

The door to the funeral home was unlocked, so I went in. I didn't find anyone to ask, so I found the restroom and changed clothes. Black pants, white shirt, necktie, shined shoes, and gray sport coat. I thought I made quite a dashing figure. If not, I was sure Claudia would let me know.

I sat for a while in the vestibule and then walked around to look things over. Mom was laid out in the main room, a nice room that would probably hold a hundred people. Her casket was open, and she looked as good as I had seen her look over the past twenty years. For some reason, seeing her didn't bother me one bit. All the flowers and plants Claudia had ordered were there too.

As I was walking back to the vestibule, I noted two stands with signature books on them. One was at each door to the main room. I went over to take a look to see if people had already stopped by to pay their respects.

I went cold with anger as I looked at the first page in the book. This page gave my Mom's lineage and details of her death. I was listed as a son and Nick as a grandchild. There was no mention of Beth or the other kids. Claudia had been at work. I should have known; she had said that she was not used to not getting her way. I ripped the lineage page out of each book and took the books back to the vestibule with me and waited.

A few people trickled in. Before long, in came Claudia and Joe with the minister.

I met them at the door.

"Why Max, you look great," Claudia said. "By the way, I don't think you've met Reverend Gatsby. Reverend, this is Max, Pearl's son."

Ignoring the reverend, I said, "Claudia, you're a bitch. You couldn't have your way with the obituary, so you thought you would try with the guest books."

Holding them in my hands I continued, "I ripped the lineage pages out. Now if you want people to sign them without any reference to me, go ahead."

I tossed the books at Joe.

"Max, I told you your mom did not want Beth and your other kids mentioned. I have to do as she wished. You know one of those books is for you."

Joe touched Claudia's elbow. She yanked it away. Reverend Gatsby looked like he didn't know what to do with himself.

"Claudia, you are full of shit. You are doing this because you don't want to be shown up for losing the obituary argument. This show is not for Mom. It's your extravaganza. It's all about Claudia and how she can show off to the citizens of Carbon. Show them what a great person she has been to poor old Pearlie. You take the fucking books. While you're at it, shove the one meant for me up your ass and make a mystery out of it. Fuck you. Keep away from me."

The reverend and Joe just stood there with mouths agape. *I bet Joe has wanted to talk that way to Claudia for years.*

I walked back into the room where the service was about to start and looked around for familiar faces. Mama Grace was there. Diana and Terry were sitting near the back of the room. They gave me a wave and flashed smiles. Aside from that, I wasn't sure if I knew anyone or not. That was until Mr. Loudmouth and his two friends arrived. It made me smile as they were seated and looked over at me sitting in the family section. I wondered if they recognized me from the counter at Barry's this morning.

Reverend Gatsby opened with a prayer and then began the service.

165

"We are gathered here today to mourn the passing of Pearl Ellis, one of Carbon's most upstanding citizens. Pearl never told a lie, she was always kind and looked out for the downtrodden, she was humble to her core, and was a friend to all mankind regardless of race, religion, or stature in our community."

I see you gave him CliffsNotes, Mom.

"One of the things Pearl wants everyone here to know is the importance of a good name. In fact, her husband, Ed, adopted Pearl's son, Max, to give him a good name."

You just had to drag me into this, didn't you?

"Let's bow our heads and thank the Lord as He welcomes Pearlie to heaven."

Somehow, I thought God could probably read through the bullshit and judge Pearlie based upon the type of person she really was. I doubted that He needed the reverend's help.

* * *

After the service, it was on to the cemetery. Of course, we were in the big Cadillac. It was strangely quiet. Claudia wasn't speaking to me, and, of course, that meant Joe wasn't speaking either. The silence was golden as far as I was concerned.

Once at the cemetery, Reverend Gatsby said a few prayers and then folks began walking to Claudia, Joe, and me to express their sympathy. I gave Mama Grace a big hug and kiss as she went by. Her eyes were red from crying. I found it hard to believe that she could feel sorrow for a woman who had treated her so poorly.

Diana and Terry stopped by.

"Thank you both again for all you've done for me," I said. Diana gave me a kiss and walked off teary eyed. Terry hugged me for the longest time and then said, "I love you, bro." Those few words meant more to me than any-one will ever know.

As the procession of people continued, I noticed Mr. Loudmouth and his two friends approaching. Loud-mouth was in the lead. He reached Claudia, said a few words, and gave her a hug. As he finished, Claudia turned to me and in her most cheerful voice said, "Max, I'm sure you remember Ted Nicholls. He was one of your dad's oldest clients."

Mr. Nicholls smiled and stuck out his hand.

Instantly, I thought back to the Wichita Police station and Sgt. Lester telling me, "Max always remember, never give wimpy handshakes."

I grabbed Loudmouth's hand and squeezed it for all I was worth. I not only squeezed it, I ground his knuckles.

He grimaced and fell to one knee.

I bent over and said, "Yes, I remember Mr. Nicholls. I heard him talking this morning at Barry's. Do you remem-ber me, sir? If not, I bet you will now."

I gave his hand one more squeeze. He looked up at me. His look said, Barry's? What the hell did I say?

As his two friends helped him to his feet, I bent over again, smiled, and said, "Fuck you from a no-good son of a bitch, Mr. Nicholls."

* * *

After another fifteen minutes, it was all over and people began to leave. I hung around the open grave site until the cemetery workers came to remove the flowers and pre-pare the casket for internment. This was the moment I had waited for, and I was not going to leave until I saw it. It took a while, but the workers lowered the casket. Then my moment arrived: One of the workers began to pitch dirt into the open grave.

That was all I needed. I was convinced I was free at last.

Not a tear. Not a tear when Victor died. Not a tear at Ed's funeral. And not a tear at Mom's funeral. Not crying at these occasions was not something I was necessarily proud of, but I wondered what it meant about me as a person. *Maybe someday some psychiatrist can explain that to me.*

A short ride back to the mortuary, a change of clothes, a sandwich, and one more chore. Then I would be out of Carbon and on to Wichita and then home.

* * *

The sign on the window said **Jonathan Cottonfeld, Esq. Attorney at Law.** I pulled the hog into the parking stall and killed the engine. I was a little late. The meeting was set for 2:00 p.m., and it was almost ten past. I swung off the bike and entered the office.

"Hi, I'm Max Ellis, and I have a meeting with John—I mean Mr. Cottenfeld," I said to the receptionist.

"Yes, Mr. Ellis. Please follow me."

Jonathan, Claudia, Jim, and Mama Grace were already seated in the conference room.

"Sorry to hold you folks up, but I had a couple of things to take care of," I said.

"Well, I believe that all are present and accounted for now. Let's begin," said Jonathan.

Jonathan spent the next several minutes explaining his position as Mom's attorney, Claudia's position as executor, and the items he wanted to cover in this meeting.

"The will, as Ms. Ellis wished, is divided into three parts for the heirs: Ms. Grace DeLong, Mr. Maxwell Ellis, and lastly, Ms. Claudia Peters. Following Ms. Ellis' desires, I will address each heir in that order."

"Ms. DeLong, Ms. Ellis wanted to acknowledge your true and faithful service with a check in the amount of twenty thousand dollars. She also wants you to have a number of Mr. Edward Ellis' office furnishings. She knew how much you thought of Mr. Ellis and thought you would enjoy these items. Ms. Peters is charged with delivering the furnishings to you within thirty days. Here is the check for twenty thousand dollars made out to you."

"Why, thank you, Mr. Cottenfeld. It was most gracious of Ms. Ellis to think of me in this way," said Mama Grace. She dabbed her eyes.

Mama Grace was being more than gracious. I felt my temperature rise but stayed quiet. *Furniture and a measly twenty grand! They owe her more than that. She was treated more like a servant than an employee.*

"Now for Mr. Ellis. To begin with, your mother wanted me to give you this."

Out of his desk drawer came a legal-sized manila envelope. I couldn't believe it. Damned if the woman wasn't reaching out from the grave to give me one more poison pen letter. The envelope wasn't sealed, so I opened it. Sure enough, typed sideways on legal-sized paper was a letter. I skipped to the last page without reading it. The last page was page thirteen, and on it was her signature.

I couldn't help it. I started to laugh.

"Do you want to let us in on the joke, Max?" Jonathan said.

No more Mr. Ellis. Now it's Max. He knew what was in the letter. I was sure he had read it.

"Perhaps you would like to read us some of the letter from your mother, Max," he said.

"No, *Johnny*. I don't think I need to do that." His eyes flashed, but he didn't protest.

"I've received many of these legal-sized epistles," I said.

"I think I will do with this what I've done with the rest over the years."

I tore the letter up, page by page, and placed the pieces on his desk.

"Well, let's move on, shall we," the attorney said as he tried to regain his composure.

"Your mother acknowledged to me that many years ago you were disowned by both she and Ed. They also took out emancipated minor papers on you. From what she said, you were never happy with the good name of Ellis and stated on many occasions your desire to have nothing to do with your parents. She also said that you made it abundantly clear that you did not want or need their money or properties. Do you hereby acknowledge that those statements of your mother's are true?"

"Yes, I do. But what does that have to do with her will, and why am I here?"

"Patience, Mr. Ellis."

Oh, we're back to Mr. Ellis. I better bend over and spread some Vaseline. Here comes another zinger.

"Your mother wants to find out if you're the hypocrite she thinks you to be. I have here a check for fifty thousand. It is made out to you. You said you were above taking their money. Are you really? Your mother wanted to bet me that you would fold and take the money when presented with a check. If you do not take it, the money will go to Claudia to do with as she chooses. Your mother also suggested that if you were to take the money, you should donate it to her favorite charities. In her name of course. A list of acceptable charities will be provided if you elect that option. What will it be, Max?"

I looked around the room. Old John boy was smiling like he had me by the balls and was enjoying it. Mama

Grace was looking like she wanted to be anywhere but in that room. Claudia looked like she had just peed her pants at the thought of losing $50,000. Joe looked like he just wanted this charade over.

I stood up and walked over to John.

"John, is this the last bullshit item you have for me?"

"If you call fifty thousand dollars bullshit, then yes it is."

"Okay. I'll tell you what I am going to do. I'm going to take the money," I said.

Claudia let out a gasp, and Johnny cracked a shit-eating grin.

I grabbed the check from his hand, took a pen off the desk, and endorsed it in front of them all.

"Now before you call me a hypocrite or any other name, let me tell you why I took the money and what I'm going to do with it."

"We don't need to know all of that, Max. You've just proven yourself a hypocrite," John said.

"Shut the fuck up, John, and listen."

He sat back in his overstuffed office chair and looked at me standing over him.

"Yes, folks. I'm taking the money. What I am going to do with it is give it all to a little lady that gave so much to Pearl and Ed. A lady that was given furniture instead of retirement payments after years of faithful service. Mama Grace, I want you to have this for your retirement."

"But Max, I can't take this money. It's yours from your mother."

"No, Mama. You take it. Use it for your retirement. Use it for your church. Buy choir robes or new hymnals, I don't care. You'll put it to good use for others. If Claudia gets it, well, you can only imagine how she would use it."

No one said a word, so I went on.

"Now Mama, I want you to promise to do me a favor. I want you to make two donations with a little of that money. The first donation is to go to the Catholic Church. Mom hated the Catholics and spoke against them so often that I think they deserve a donation from her. The second donation is to go to Planned Parenthood. That only seems appropriate as Mom would probably rue the day I was born if she could be here today. Both of those donations should be made in the name of Mrs. Pearl Ellis."

The Planned Parenthood thing brought another gasp from Claudia.

"Mama Grace, will you promise to do those things for me?" I asked.

She reluctantly nodded her head. I knew if she said yes, she would do it.

I turned back to the attorney.

"Well, John. Good to see ya again. I think I'll be on my way now. You all take care."

I turned and walked out the door before anyone else could speak. I felt good about what I had done. I felt that my honor and scruples had shown through. I was proud of myself.

* * *

I gassed up on the way out of town. No one was at the pump to make any negative comments or give me any trouble this time.

The hog sounded good, and the air smelled clean as I left town. Carbon was a good little town full of a lot of stand-up people. I wondered if I would ever come back to visit.

Next stop Wichita, then on home.

I left Carbon with a great hope that this trip was going to bring me the closure I sought. The years of hatred had worn me down.

Chapter 21

After returning home, life returned to normal. But the fact that she was dead and buried had not done much to diminish the hatred I felt toward my mother. Not having phone calls from her or multi-page, typed letters to piss me off did make life easier. I didn't think of her as often, but the abuse I had experienced was always near the surface. I did my best not to dwell on it.

* * *

Six months after Mom's funeral, I drove up to the house after work and spotted two boxes on my front porch. Walking up to the porch, I noticed the handwriting on the labels attached to the boxes. My blood ran cold. *Claudia!*

I had only heard from her once since I returned from the funeral. She had written to tell me how she and Joe were cleaning out Mom's house. They were going to sell it soon. She went on to tell me about the two farms Mom had left her. Claudia said that Mom's instructions in the will were to keep the farms at all costs. Mom said she wanted the farms to remain in the family forever.

It had to bother Claudia that she couldn't liquidate them. She was anything but a farm girl. Money, position, and power was what she wanted.

I was just glad I'd been able to screw her out of that $50,000. I still laughed about the donations to the Catholic Church and Planned Parenthood. I hoped that Claudia was still fuming over those gifts.

Apparently, Joe and Claudia were going to continue

to see that the western Kansas farm was maintained as a tenant farm. However, she had grand plans for the Bradley farm. She was going to redo all the buildings and turn it into a hunting preserve for Joe.

I had thought, *How Claudia that is—a hunting preserve.* I thought "hunting" and "preserve" were contradictory terms.

I carried the two boxes into the garage and set them on the work bench. They weren't big boxes, about 2 by 1 by 1 foot. They reminded me of a box a grocery store might use for apples.

I took a knife from the work bench to open them and then suddenly stopped.

What were in those boxes anyway? Sure, they were from Claudia. But what the hell would she have sent? I was sure that if it had been something of value, she would have kept that for herself.

I went over to the beer fridge, grabbed a cold one, and sat down at the workbench to think.

The more I thought about it, I didn't want to open them. I was sure they contained nothing good. Since the funeral, I had spent a lot of effort trying to bury the past. I didn't need whatever was in those boxes to open up old wounds or, for that matter, create new ones.

I sat drinking my beer and looking at them.

When Beth came home from work, I showed her the boxes and told her I didn't think I wanted to open them.

"If you don't want to open them, then don't," she said. "Just put them in the attic. Someday maybe you will want to see what's in them. If it is just more poison from your mom, the attic is just the place for them.

"Now, what shall we do for dinner?" she asked.

The boxes went to the attic where they remained unopened for years.

Chapter 22

Being a couple of years past sixty, retirement was just around the corner, and it scared the hell out of me. I had opened a local engineering office for a national firm and walked several days a week during the noon hour. The office was in a nice complex along a river, so a nice mid-day walk was always enjoyable.

On one of these walks, I was trying to plot out a strategy for retirement and nearly ran over a lady as she exited a small office building. I excused myself and continued but noted the name of the office the lady had just left: Horizon Counseling Center.

Once back in my office, I thought back to Irene Wilson, the counselor I had enjoyed so much years before.

I looked up Horizon's phone number and dialed.

"Hello, Horizon Counseling Center," a woman on the other end of the phone with a very nice voice said.

"Yes, my name is Max Ellis, and I have a few questions if you have a minute."

"Why yes, I do. I'm Dr. Shakespeare. How may help you?"

"I am just about at retirement age, and, frankly, I'm not looking forward to it. I don't know what I am going to do with myself. Do you ever work with people like me?"

"Yes, I do. Yours is not an uncommon concern. I would suggest that we have an initial consultation to see if I can help you. I assume you are working still, so when might you be available to come in?"

I was sold. This would be good. I'd get some good ideas, and I could roll into retirement.

* * *

"Max, hello. It's nice to meet you." A beautiful, young blond just over 5 feet tall and pregnant as could be greeted me. She looked like she had swallowed a beach ball!

She showed me into her office. It was apparent immediately that I was dealing with one smart lady.

"So, Max. Tell me about yourself and how you feel about your career and retirement." she said.

"I think I've accomplished most of the things I set out to do in my career, and it has long been a tenet of mine that at some time you should get out of the way, and let the next generation come along with new ideas. I've heard a number of old guys nearing the end of their careers tell the young pup engineers why they couldn't do something: 'It has always been done that way, and, damn it, you young guys should not question that.' I do not want to be one of those guys."

"Many people retire because they're tired of what they're doing. It's nice to hear a reason like yours," she responded. "Tell me about your hobbies."

"I've worked so long that I don't know what I'll do. I am a terrible golfer, so that's out. Beth and I really don't enjoy travelling. All the kids and grandkids are within fifty miles of home, so we don't need to travel. I don't have a bunch of hobbies either. I do like computers and electronics, but that won't keep me entertained full-time."

"Are you up for some homework?" Jessica asked.

"Sure. What are you thinking?"

"Before we meet again, I'd like you to go to a few hobby and craft shops to look at what they carry. See if anything strikes your fancy."

"Sounds easy enough," I said.

* * *

The following week, Jessica greeted me with an enthusiastic smile.

"Nice to see you again, Max. How'd it go at the hobby shops?"

"Well, none of those places held any interest. No model airplanes or ships for me. We could also forget carpentry and woodworking. I'm pretty sure that whatever I would make would turn out to be a what-not shelf. I think I need to widen my search, but it was a good exercise in *you gotta know what you don't wanna do as well as what you wanna do.*"

* * *

The more we talked, the more Jessica probed into my past. Before long I was relating my story: Mom, Victor, and Ed. We discussed my dissatisfaction at home, my leaving Carbon, hitchhiking, bumming around the country, the service and Vietnam. We even got into my marriages to Jane and Beth.

"Max, you've talked about how much you love your career and said something about how your mom didn't want you to become an engineer. Dentist, right?" Jessica asked.

"Yes, she wanted to be able to tell people I was Dr. Max Ellis. It was all about show for her. It never mattered what I wanted," I said.

"I'm sensing a lot of rage, Max. Would it be helpful to talk about it?" she asked. "You can tell me whatever's on your mind. I'm not a judge. I care about you and am here to help you move into the next phase of your life with a sense of joy and anticipation rather than dread. And I'm concerned that if you can't let go of that rage, it will consume you as soon as you have more time to think about it. Does that make sense?"

I had to let that sink in. Jessica sat back and gave me the space to absorb and process her words.

After a few minutes of thinking about how freeing it had been to talk to Irene, I decided to see if Jessica could help me get through my hatred once and for all. I had nothing to lose.

"You're right, and I want to be done with these feelings. I thought that when I saw the dirt on my mom's coffin, I'd be free. But it's been years since she died, and I still can't let it go."

"I'm not sure where to start, Jessica. Honestly."

"Why don't you tell me the first thing that comes to mind then."

"Well, since we're talking about death, I might as well start with the day my dad, Victor, died."

Jessica nodded and took a sip of her tea.

I slowly continued. "That night, my mom forced me sleep with her and be 'the man of the house,'" I said.

Jessica didn't blink.

"How old were you, Max?" she asked.

"About seven."

"And had that ever happened before?"

"Yes. When Victor was gone for the war … She always made me sleep in her bed," I said. "As soon as Ed and Mom got married, her bedroom antics stopped. However, she would often walk in on me while I was bathing and seemed to always catch me when I was in some state of undress. It was a real invasion of privacy. There were no locks on the bathroom doors, so I had to be careful."

"Are you okay, Max? Do you want to keep going?" I could see why Jessica was a counselor. Her chairside manner was amazing.

"I'm okay, thanks. This is not stuff I talk about, but it's not like it's not on my mind. I still have dreams about the early days when I had to share a bed with her, and she made me act as the man of the house. Those memories are so uncomfortable and distasteful that I often wake up in sweats. At times, I doubt that those things happened. But the memories are too vivid to dismiss."

"That's a common reaction to that kind of abuse, Max. I can help you through it."

"I really appreciate it. It's hard, but it's time. I'll do whatever I need to do."

Chapter 23

"Last time I saw you, we talked about your father's death and your mother's inappropriate behavior until your stepdad came into the picture. Do you mind telling me more about your relationship with your mother after she and Ed got married?" Jessica asked.

"One thing I didn't mention last time was that even though I was no longer man of the house after Mom and Ed got married, she still made me kiss her on the mouth and emphasized loving your mother. Love your mother. Love your mother. But I *hated* the kissing on the mouth and the way she acted around my friends."

"She was inappropriate around your friends?"

"Yes. One time, I asked my buddy Dick to come over after school to play basketball. We walked into the kitchen to get something to eat. Right in plain sight was Mom doing her ironing. I thought Dick's eyes were going to pop out of his head. There stood Mom in nothing but a bra and panties!"

I shifted in my seat and looked out the window before continuing.

"My mom said hi to us, and without even covering up, said, 'What are you doing this afternoon?' Seeing Dick's uneasiness, I was quick to answer. I told her we were going to play basketball and had just stopped by to get something to eat. I told her we'd be out of there soon, but she said, 'No need to hurry,' then asked Dick how his parents were doing. She wanted to carry on a conversation in her bra and panties!"

"Mmhmm," Jessica responded.

I continued. "As soon as we were outside, Dick asked if my mom always walked around like that. I tried to make excuses, but probably did a poor job. It was embarrassing. And that wasn't the only time she'd done that. It was never clear to me why Mom wanted to show herself off like that. It just didn't fit with her obsession with women like our neighbor Georgia Mulligan and the way she had acted about other things."

"What was it about Georgia that your mom was obsessed about?"

"Money. Her looks," I said. "Two things come to mind. During one dinnertime discussions, I listened to Mom and Ed rant about the Mulligans. 'They inherited their money. They didn't have to work for it like you did, Ed,' my mom said. Then Ed chimed in. 'That's right, Pearlie. Gary Mulligan has never done an honest day's work in his life.' Then mom started in on the way Georgia dressed. Ed—he was obsessed too in his own way—said, 'Yes, she looks pretty good. Big boobs and a nice ass!' That got mom and she said Georgia looked like a tramp in her low-cut blouses and shorts. Ed said, 'From what I've heard, she just married old Gary for his money— poor bastard. Bet he feels really bad every time he climbs in bed with her.' Mom pretended to scold him for being unkind, but I knew she agreed. She and Ed used to say that our area of town should've been named Inheritance Hill. My parents seemed obsessed with the wealth and position of these people."

I went on. "To earn money, I used to mow lawns. Mrs. Mulligan once saw me mowing her neighbor's yard and asked if I would do their yard too. Sounded like an opportunity to me. Everything went well for several weeks and then my mom happened to drive by while I was working in their yard. Mrs. Mulligan was sitting on the front porch in one of her scant outfits while I worked. That was it for my mom. I had to give up that lawn job."

"Sounds like your mom was jealous," said Jessica. By the look on her face, I knew that what I'd always felt was true, that this stuff wasn't right, that it was, indeed, *not normal.*

"Girlfriends were another strange thing. Mom always quizzing me about girls, especially the girls I showed interest in."

"What would she ask?"

"'What do her parents do?' 'Where do they live?' 'What church do they go to?' Standard questions. As I got older, the question became much more personal like 'What is their reputation?' The biggest question became 'Is she *clean*?' Clean to Mom meant do they fool around, and is she a virgin? Again with the sexual stuff. Mom had a big fixation on anything having to do with sex. Through junior high and high school, Mom tried to fix me up with girls that met her criteria. Not only did I not know those girls, but there was no way I would let my mother choose my girlfriends."

I looked at my watch. *Fifteen more minutes. I'm in this far; I may as well keep going.*

"On one occasion, I made the mistake of bringing one of my girlfriends up during a conversation at the dinner table. 'Max, are you saying you like that girl? I want you to know that her family are nobodies and are definitely not *our* kind of people.' And what kind of people are *our* kind of people, Mom, I asked. She said, 'Well certainly not her kind. I think they are even Catholic, and I have heard stories about that Jennifer. She's loose and most assuredly not clean.' Ed just sat there and let her rant. Mom just kept

182

going. She accused this poor girl of being willing to do anything to get the Ellis name, even get herself pregnant."

"Learning about and beginning to experiment with sexual things were awkward for me. My experiences with my mother had my sexuality totally out of sync. I was so tired of being asked almost daily if I was still clean—that I had not screwed some girl, or for that matter, even come close to screwing some girl. I wanted to be anything but clean; however, I had such a skewed view of sex that I was fearful about how to handle myself.

"I had dates throughout high school. Dates with girls *I* selected. I did my share of kissing and feeling around, but that was my limit. Beyond that seemed somehow dirty and was a place I could not go. The early incest experiences had taken their toll on me. What had happened in the past was not something I would discuss with anyone; those feelings would have to remain suppressed. I kept thinking: Don't think about it, don't talk about it, get out of the house and out from under her thumb, it will all go away. Keep everything compartmentalized. It will be better when I am out on my own, even interaction with girls will be better when I get away from this place. Then I can forget my past experiences and learn what I need to know. The key—get out of that place as soon as possible!"

Jessica just listened. I've never seen someone look so comfortable listening for so long. For the first time, I was able to let it out, get it all off my chest. No filter, no guilt. No tears. *Well, that part hasn't changed.*

"Throughout my senior year I did sometimes question my desire to leave. I kept watching my friends. I would see them having strong relationships with their family members. I would see the loving and mutual respect between my friends and their parents. This made me question that something must be wrong with me. I'd watch my parents interface with other people in Carbon. While they didn't seem to have many close friends, they did have a lot of acquaintances. These people all seemed to enjoy Ed's stupid jokes and related well with my mother.

"I just couldn't understand why people couldn't see Pearl and Ed as I did. A couple of phonies who would cut you to pieces as soon as you turned your back. A couple who would use you whenever possible and go to extremes to make you feel obligated to them. I just kept wondering why people didn't see what was going on. I unfairly blamed the people of Carbon for not seeing my parents as I saw them.

"All of these thoughts made we wonder if I was the one who was off. I felt like such a fish out of water. I also wondered just where I got my ideals and beliefs. I certainly hadn't taken after my mother. Maybe I was like my father? But then I'd think No, he was a no-good alcoholic. So, I wondered, who do I take after?"

Chapter 24

"Tell me more about Ed and how he and your mother parented you," Jessica said.

"Getting older, I began to ask questions about the things I remembered. I asked Mom for details about the Maddux family, my dad's family. This was always met with an angry response. She'd say, 'Max, I've told you a hundred times. The Maddux name is not to be mentioned. You are an Ellis now; do not mention those people.'

"She'd say, 'You have a good name now. A respected name. You need to be grateful for that name and thank Ed for it occasionally.' There was the name thing again. I got to where I would bring up the Madduxes just to get under her skin. The problem I have now is that she's still under mine. I hate her. I've hated her for over fifty years."

"Max, I don't think your issue is really hatred. It sounds to me like you've suppressed your feelings about life issues you've faced and are calling it hatred rather than dealing directly with your feelings."

That was not the first time I had been accused of not being in touch with my feelings. Irene had told me that years before.

Jessica continued. "My goal is to help you get in touch with your feelings, so you can grasp how these life events have impacted you. If you can get there, then perhaps you can address the events and the people behind them in a more rational way. Forgiveness is what I want you to understand. That's forgiveness of the individuals, *not* the acts. I also want to help you get to the point where you can forgive yourself."

I thought, This is bullshit. Jessica can go piss up a rope. I'm not about to forgive those assholes for the shit they put me through! I really do not have anything to forgive myself for. I'm the one who's been wronged!

But I respected her, so I hung in there, not as a true believer but more out of interest as to where she was trying to guide me.

"Alright. I'll try to do that, but I don't think I really have anything to forgive myself for," I responded.

"Thank you, Max. Are you willing to do another homework assignment?"

"Sure."

"What I'd like for you to do is write a few letters. The purpose behind these letters is to … in a safe way … go back in time and express yourself. As you express yourself in a letter, you are not going into the experience as a participant; you're going in as an observer. Also, you're going in with all the resources you have today in the here and now, resources you didn't have back when you were originally going through the experience. You are able to manage the situation much better with the tools you have today. It is important to remember as you write, this event can never happen again."

I nodded and let her continue.

"Letter writing allows you to fuse your adult self with the child self and be in touch with your feelings. Please remember, every time you write a letter to somebody else, the requirement that has to be met before you send that letter is that you have no expectations in return. You can send off the letter, and it really doesn't matter what the other person says or does. Many of the statements you will say in the letters are expressions of how you *feel*, or you are telling someone how they are personally impacting you. The letter is for you. For you to be able to *feel*.

"Sometimes people avoid self-disclosure like this because they feel vulnerable; they feel like somebody will take that information and use it against them. But if you're not expecting your words to be validated, or legitimized by another, this method will work. It's not about being right and wrong; it's about being understood for who you are."

I nodded. It made head sense, but it also made me uncomfortable.

"It sounds very black and white," she continued, "but it's very emotional. Validation comes only when you are empowered to advocate for what you want from a relationship knowing that you are only one part of the two or more in that relationship. Your mother never learned this, and she also never learned that she could not control other people. So, if you try to address your hatred with forgiveness, you will know you have done your very best. Truth and forgiveness are what will make you free and remove the hatred."

* * *

Jessica had me journal along with writing numerous letters. Often the letters were to dead people and would never be sent. All the writing did help. I felt freer, and I thought I was more in touch with my feelings relating to the events we worked on.

As we talked and I wrote and learned more about myself, I became more accepting about my life. We talked about Victor. His drunkenness, what drove him to drink, his childhood, his death, and his lasting impact on me.

We discussed Ed and his lack of involvement in my life, how all he could do was joke, his ability to shirk his role as a father, and about his relationship with Mom. We discussed Vietnam and its long-term impact on me. What it had been like to be alone on the highway hitchhiking away from Carbon as a seventeen-year-old. We discussed my marriage to Jane and the many happy years I had now with Beth and the kids. We discussed my career and the enjoyment I had with the projects I had the opportunity to work on.

One of the first letters I wrote and actually sent was to Claudia. I did my best to not argue but simply explain what had happened during my childhood and why I had such a hatred for my mother. I was explicit, sharing the details. It didn't take long for a response.

Claudia said she could not believe me and chastised me for even thinking such things about my mother let alone writing them down. My response was quick and without anger. I explained that it was not important that she agree with me. What was important was that I told her *why* I had the feelings I had.

That effort did not end with healing our relationship. Rather, it nearly severed it.

* * *

Jessica and I settled into our chairs as she asked, "So, Max, how do you feel about Claudia's response?"

"I am totally okay with it. I was honest with her and feel no guilt or animosity toward her. It's a wonderful feeling, a feeling I can live with," I replied.

"That's great! I'm so glad this exercise is helping you."

"I'll be honest. At first, I was just going along with it out of curiosity. I'm glad I stuck it out," I said. "But I still feel a lot of resentment over the Ellis name. I'm over sixty. I can't go out and change my name back now. It's too late."

"Let's talk through it then," Jessica prompted.

"After Mom told me she and Ed were getting married, I asked Mom about my grandmother—my dad's mom—Lissie. I wondered how I'd be able to keep in touch with her and the rest of my dad's family. That angered her. She told me we were through with them. Their names weren't to be mentioned anymore. She said that my family was now the Ellis family, not the Maddux family. She told me that Ed was going to legally adopt me and that my name was going to change. That would be the end of the Madduxes in our lives. She said, 'Remember that, Max. I don't want any of the Maddux names mentioned in front of Ed. You got that? It's important.'"

"She wanted to change everything. She said, 'Ed is going to legally adopt you. That means that all of your records will be changed, even your birth certificate. Victor will no longer be shown as your father. Ed will be. To do this we need to choose a new name for you. Your name needs to change to get rid of your middle and last name. What do you think we should do?'"

My name had been Maxwell Victor Maddux. I wanted to go with Ronald Johnson after my best friend at school, but Mom said, 'No. It has to be unique to you. Tell you what, I picked Maxwell myself. So, let's stay with that. As for the middle name let's use Purdy. That's Ma Bess and Pa Bill's name. It's also my maiden name. Your last name will be Ellis just like Ed's and mine. Now that makes Maxwell Purdy Ellis. I like it, Max. What do you think?'

"I thought it stunk and told her so. She didn't seem to care at all. She said, 'It will be Maxwell Purdy Ellis, and you will like it. Ed is giving you a good name, and that's very important. The name of Purdy is a well-respected name in Kansas. You owe your mother and new father the respect to carry this new name with honor. Remember, you owe us. We've saved you from the Maddux name.' I had lost my name and half my family, and even though she asked me what I thought, she wasn't really interested."

"Why don't you write a letter about how that made you feel too. We can discuss it during our next appointment," Jessica said.

"That reminds me. I have a business trip coming up, to Kansas if you can believe it. So, I'll have to schedule our next appointment for after I get back. Since I'm going out there, I'm going to make a side trip to Tennessee to visit my Aunt Rachel. She's actually my dad's sister and the only person who showed any interest in or concern for me at his funeral.

"I looked her up years ago, and we've been in contact by letter, phone, and email for many years," I added.

"That's great, Max. I look forward to hearing all about your trip when I see you in a few weeks."

* * *

After finishing my business, I took some time and went to Wichita to find my father's grave. That turned out to be more emotional than my mother's funeral. I thought I remembered which cemetery but was not entirely sure. I went through the cemetery records and there was not a Harry Victor Maddux listed. I could find his mother, Melissa, and his father, Harry, but no Harry Jr. Finally, after visiting his parent's actual graves, I found my father's.

* * *

"Rachel, it's so good to see you," I said as she welcomed me into her home. She exuded the same warmth and attention I remembered from the day my father died.

"Thank you so much for having me," I said as we settled into comfortable chairs in her well-lit living room. "I want to know more about Victor. I certainly did not have many of my mom's values but wonder if I have some of his. I'm hoping you can help me."

"Of course, Max. I'll do what I can."

"Most of what I know about my dad came from what my mother told me and what little memory I have of him. I always thought of Victor as an asshole, but I've never met anybody that's *all* bad. I'm hoping you can fill me in on at least a few redeeming qualities of the man and maybe give me a better view into his life and why he was the way he was."

"One thing I've come to believe is that your father was manic depressive, and I think the drinking and his mental health issues were related and not helped by his acrimonious relationship with our father," she said.

"Victor never would march to our father's drum. Dad was the city engineer in Wichita. He wanted Victor to follow in his footsteps as an engineer. But Victor wanted to study music; that was his real interest. Music was his love and passion. But he was sent off to college to be an engineer," she continued.

"Interesting. I wonder what both of them would think about me choosing to be an engineer," I said.

"I think he'd be proud of you, Max. You resisted familial pressure to become something you didn't want to be, and you're happy with that choice."

That gave me a renewed sense of pride and a real connection, an emotional connection, to my dad, something I'd never experienced.

Rachel went on. "As you might imagine, he failed miserably at college and had to return home. It was at that time that he began drinking. I suspect the hard drinking was a result of failing at college and the strained relationship with our dad. I'm convinced that it was at that time when Victor's manic-depressive symptoms began to show."

"That's interesting. No one's ever said anything about that, but it makes sense."

"I don't think anyone thought about it back then. It's only been through watching the mental health struggles some of our other family members have had that it's dawned on me that his behavior in many ways matches theirs. Of course, poor relationships, broken dreams, and war could also explain it. In some ways, he seemed hell-bent on killing himself."

Rachel got up to adjust the shades to shield our eyes from the late afternoon sun. I watched her and felt a warm sense of comfort. We'd gotten fairly close since reconnecting although we'd never gone this deep into our shared family history.

As she sat back down, I said, "Before I came to see you, I went to visit his grave and saw that his name was Henry Victor Maddux. I didn't even know his correct name; that's how lost I am and demonstrates how well my mother buried information about him. Do you know that the only picture I have of him is the one you sent me years ago, the one of him right after the war?"

"I'm sorry to hear that, Max. But I'm glad I had that one to give you."

"Me too. You know, I've often toyed with the idea of changing my name back to Maddux." I paused, then continued. "However, I didn't want to do it just out of revenge to my mother. I only wanted to do it if it would make a difference in how I felt about myself."

"Max, a person's character is not defined by a name but by the kind of person they are."

In the end, I decided to leave my name as Ellis.

* * *

"Welcome home, honey," Beth said as I opened the garage door and stepped into the kitchen. "How was your trip?"

I grabbed one of the fresh cookies she'd stacked on a plate, her way of letting me know she was glad I was home. "Good, really good," I said.

I kissed her on the forehead, set down my bag, and pulled out a stool. "You might think this is crazy, but I've come up with a solution to my name issue. I'm going to get Maxwell Victor Maddux tattooed across my back."

"I do think you're crazy, but if that's what you need to do then I support you."

I grabbed a scratch pad and a stubby pencil from the junk drawer and said, "Come here. I'll show you what I'm thinking."

Beth looked over my shoulder as I sketched my shoulders and back and wrote MAXWELL VICTOR MADDUX in big letters that stretched from shoulder to shoulder. Under the name, I added a rather large barbed wire design. "I like the barbed wire. It seems a very nice touch."

"But you won't be able to see it," Beth said.

"What matters to me is that it's there, that it's bold and that I'll die with that name. By having the tattoo, I'll feel like I have recaptured the years I lost as a result of the name change to Ellis."

Chapter 25

"Hi, Max. Nice to see you again. How was your trip?" Jessica asked as she settled into her chair. I leaned back in mine but was quickly reminded that just a few days earlier, I'd rewritten my identity with new ink. I shifted forward slightly and got Jessica caught up.

"Now that you know more about your dad and his up-bringing and how that can have—as you're well aware—a profound effect on a person's life, what do you know about your mother's early life?"

"A lot. Mom always delighted in telling of her exploits as a child. She grew up on a farm near Bradley, Kansas. Mom's parents, Bill and Bessie Purdy, had moved to Kansas from Illinois shortly after getting married. Bill was apparently a very enterprising man. He immediately put a down payment on a farm and began to make it pay. Over the years Bill also started a gas station in Bradley, the first one. He joined with some other farmers and started the only bank in town. My grandparents had been married about eight years when my mom was born. Two other children died in infancy.

"Ma Bess never talked much about mom as a child. How-ever, Mom would often talk about her time on the farm as the greatest time of her life. She always talked about how much she had loved her father. She often bragged about how she'd had him wrapped around her little finger. 'There was nothing that I wanted that Pa Bill wouldn't get for me,' she would tell me.

"Apparently, she was a good-looking young lady too. She and Ma Bess had both told me how Mom had won the Miss Bradley contest when she was eighteen. The way they made it sound, I thought that was as big as the Miss America Pageant. Mom had also played the piano in the small movie house in Bradley.

"From what I understand, Bradley in her day had a population of about three hundred and consisted of a one-block business district. Pa Bill was a big thing in Bradley. Mom used to tell me that most of those people who remained in Bradley after the Depression owed their survival to Pa Bill in some way. Mom thought having someone owe you showed you were a success.

"She also often told me about all the boyfriends she had during her days in Bradley. The one I heard the most about was Lavette Van something or other. It seems Lavette was from a wealthy farming family and chased my mother all during high school. She would never let him catch her. He was overweight and not very good-looking, she said. She would often lament that if she had chosen Lavette instead of Victor, we'd have been rich.

"After high school, Pa Bill sent Mom to Wichita to business college. In those days, only the wealthy girls went to college. The fact that the Depression was in full swing made it even more of a rarity. Mom didn't talk a lot about her time there, but I did pick up a few things from some of her friends, Peg and LaVonne.

"After Victor died, Peg and LaVonne would come to visit Mom. They would all sit in the living room and tell stories about their single days. Sometimes their voices would get low, almost a whisper. Then they would laugh, never explaining to me what they had said that was so funny. Once they were telling a story about a monkey. It sounded like they were beating the monkey. When Mom saw that I was listening, she stopped the conversation and sent me out of the room. I never learned what happened to the monkey, but I did hear something about a doctor being needed.

"All I know for sure is that Mom graduated from college and went to work for the Federal Land Bank. She worked there for almost ten years before she married. Somewhere along the line she met my dad. I'm not sure how that happened exactly, but I think it had something to do with their shared interest in music.

"My impression is that Victor was the partier that Pearl enjoyed, and Pearl had the responsible job that Victor admired. They dated for several years. Probably the events that made all of this possible were the deaths of their fathers. They both died within months of one another, and both my mom and dad came into some money. That money allowed them to continue their partying lifestyle until 1942. Victor was a hot item for the draft. Lissie tried to pull every political string she could, but it didn't work. My parents married just before he shipped out for basic training."

"It sounds like you've done quite a bit of research," Jessica said.

"Most of what I know is from conversations I overheard between Lissie and my mom and things I heard my mom discuss with Peg and LaVonne. Ma Bess never spoke about those times. I never understood why."

"That's very interesting, Max. That means your mom would have been in her teens in the late twenties, early thirties. There's a good body of research that shows a high rate of pedophilia and sexual abuse during those years. The highest rate appeared to have occurred in rural areas, like farming communities. According to the studies, it wasn't uncommon for young girls to have been molested by their fathers. There were few checks and balances in those years. I also think, based on other things you've said, that it's highly likely that your mom was pregnant when she married your dad."

I had not considered either of these things. But as we worked through it, things began to make sense. And if she had been abused by her father it would partially explain what she had done to me. She had been a victim too!

But I still hate her!

"This is all supposition, of course," Jessica added. "To be clear though, I am convinced that your mom was indeed a pedophile. None of that excuses her actions. It only perhaps explains *why* she was the way she was."

She went on. "Forgiveness, forgiveness is for individuals, not the for the acts they perpetrate."

Just when I thought we had covered everything, I remembered the boxes. The boxes that had been in my attic, unopened for over seventeen years. The boxes I feared opening. Those boxes. I told Jessica about them.

"Max, you must open those. They may open a new world for you and provide a much fuller insight into your parents' lives. They could be a treasure. Why are they still in the attic after all these years?"

"Jessica, the boxes are where they belong. My guess is that they are filled with more poison from my mom. You know about her legal-sized letters. You've even read some of them. No, I have no great desire to open those boxes."

"Max, you're wrong!" she said. "We need to work toward opening those boxes. These could hold the key to the door to forgiveness."

I should have known I would lose the argument. We started journaling about the boxes and writing more letters. One of them proved to be the hardest one to complete.

"Max, I want you to write a letter to a young Max. The purpose of the letter is to explain to young Max what his life will be like. Explain the abuse, the heartache, the loneliness he will experience. I also want you to provide him with a roadmap for how to navigate those obstacles. Will you do that?"

"Yes, I'll do it," I said reluctantly.

* * *

I spent several weeks drafting that letter. It was difficult for me to find the right words to properly express the experiences and my feelings.

When the letter was complete, Jessica issued a challenge.

"Max, I want you to go home and pick a time to open those boxes. You should climb up into the attic. Don't hurry with this task. Think it through. Once you're up there, I want you to contemplate what you are about to do. You are about to learn about your life. Take your time. In fact, take a pillow up there and stay awhile. Once you have thought through what you hope to see in those boxes, I want you to read the letter to young Max. Read it out loud, so the words resonate with you. When you've done that, open the boxes."

She continued, "Please remember, it doesn't actually matter what's in them. No matter what the items are, they are part of your life. Above all, enjoy the experience."

Now it was up to me. I had no idea what awaited me.

Chapter 26

It took a few days, but I was determined to follow through. Those boxes had been in the attic for over seventeen years. I had no real idea of what they contained, but I had great trepidation about opening them.

No reason to fear the contents. What could they contain that I haven't already seen, I kept telling myself. The worst would be more letters from Mom. I'd been through many of those, so it was time to do what Jessica said: Open those boxes.

I chose a Sunday afternoon. While Beth was away at the grocery store, I gathered up a flashlight and a pillow as Jessica had suggested and headed toward the attic. I pulled the stairs down slowly and looked up into the dimly lit space before committing.

It took a while to locate the boxes. But when I found them I could still make out Claudia's writing and her Carbon address. I moved them to an area under the lone light and brushed off the layer of dust that had collected. Once that was done, I sat alone in the attic with the boxes and my thoughts, trying to find an inner peace. In case there were letters or some other items that would piss me off, I wanted to be in a position to offer forgiveness to myself and to my mother.

After sitting there for what seemed like an hour, I leaned back on the pillow, looked at the boxes, and pulled out the letter I had written to my younger self.

I hesitated and took a deep breath. *It's not going to get easier with the passage of time, so start reading.*

To young Maxwell Victor Maddux,

This is your older voice with some information that I want to share with you. Some of this will not be easy to hear or easy to understand. I'm sorry that you have to hear this. Please know that this is written with your best interests at heart.

Your father, Victor, will be serving in WWII for most of the first—

* * *

Suddenly, I felt a presence. I looked at the boxes. Behind them, I saw a vision of my mother. She was not alone. Ed, Victor, and a nondescript fellow were with her. I suppose some would call this a religious experience.

It did not feel like it had any religious significance other than the fact that the nondescript person appeared to be dressed in a robe of some kind, something like a Catholic priest would wear. All the others were dressed in street clothes. They all appeared to be middle aged just like I imaged them to look in their prime of life. I gave the nondescript person a name—the Arbiter. The Arbiter seemed to be in charge. Victor and Ed seemed in good spirits and were smiling and talking among themselves. Mom was quiet. Her head was down, and she looked uncomfortable.

My entire body was overwhelmed with sensation, and I pinched myself to make sure I was not dreaming. The experience was surreal.

Not wanting to lose the moment, I spoke to them. "I'm here because I want to read a letter I wrote to young Maxwell Victor Maddux and convey to him the importance of forgiveness and let him know that he had support no matter what." No one spoke, but the Arbiter nodded. Taking no comments as permission from all, I continued reading my letter:

Your father, Victor, will be serving in WWII for most of the first four years of your life. When he returns, he will have an alcohol problem. This problem will impact your relationship with him. Your memories of him during this time will be related to his alcohol use. He will take you to bars, physically abuse you and your mother, and you will on many occasions take care of him while he is in a drunken state. One of the strongest memories you will carry throughout your life is of the night he dies. On that night, he will be ill and ambulance drivers will come to get him. He will refuse to go and will try to put you into the car with him as he attempts to escape. The ambulance drivers will divert him and remove you from the car. Your father will become so angry that he will speed off, only to crash the car almost immediately. He will return home to bleed out during the night. Your memory of that night will include images of wiping drool from his face as he lay on the couch dying. The next day your only question regarding his death will be, "Is my name going to be in the paper?"

Your mother will do all she can to remove your memory of Victor. She will forbid contact with his family, change your name to Maxwell Purdy Ellis, and attempt to transfer your fatherly feelings to her second husband, Ed. Much later in your life, you will develop a strong relationship with your Aunt Rachel, Victor's sister. She will explain that Victor suffered from manic depression and had significant issues with his own father.

Victor felt that he had not lived up to his family's expectations. Rachel is of the opinion that Victor's perceived personal failures and his depression were key factors in his path to becoming an alcoholic.

Your mother, Pearl, will have a dramatic impact on your life. She was raised in a privileged lifestyle in a small farming community during the Depression. She will tell you that she was the apple of her father's eye. She attended college in Wichita where she met Victor. She did not marry until her early thirties. These items are mentioned because of Pearl's later actions. There may have been sexual abuse by her father, and she may have had to get married because she was pregnant. Having to get married was a terrible thing to bear in those days. While these are assumptions on my part, such events may help explain many of her actions during your early years.

Your earliest memories of Pearl will be during the time Victor is away at war. Even though you will be old enough to sleep alone, Pearl will have you sleep with her. She will take advantage of that closeness to perform acts of incest—inappropriately fondling you, forcing you to suckle her, and having you touch her.

These acts will continue, usually under the guise of "being the man of the house" until she marries her second husband, Ed. Her inappropriate sexually related actions will continue throughout your youth. She will walk around in various stages of undress, kiss you on the mouth, attempt touching, and find ways of walking in on you during times of your undress. In addition, your mother will con-

stantly stress the need for you to "love your mother," the importance of taking care of your mother,
and the evils of sexual desire.

At this point Mom began to sob. She continued to hang
her head. At no point did she contradict or argue. Not
once. I continued:

Not to excuse her actions but I believe many of
your mother's acts can be explained if you accept
that she too was a victim of child sexual abuse,
and she may have been forced to marry. While
also wrong, your mother may have seen you as a
male substitute while Victor was at war and after
he died.

For all of the things your mother will do wrong,
she will provide you with several strong personal tenets that will positively impact your life. Your
mother's actions will also result in feelings of anger
and hatred. As you grow into your teenage years,
you will continue to question your mother's sexual actions. Contradictions surrounding sex and
sexual desire will plague and confuse you for some
years.

You will wonder about Victor and if you are
like him. You will feel a father void that will not be
filled by Ed. Because of the distaste you will have
for the way you are raised, you will rebel and do
all within your power to differentiate yourself from
your mother and the Ellis lifestyle. Your approach
to distasteful things will be to suppress all bad
feelings and force them from your mind, avoiding
them entirely. You will identify many of the bad
qualities of your mother and father and go to ex-
treme lengths not to repeat them as an adult.

It will never be easy for you to find good things to say about your mother, father, or Ed. If not careful, you will live with a very black or white, right or wrong mindset.

You must learn to be forgiving—forgiving of those who have wronged you and forgiving of yourself. Be conscious to guard against any tendency to overreact to such personal ideals as self-doubt, lack of trust in others, and hard-and-fast rules for life. Be careful not to become filled with hate. Allow people to get close to you and to know you. Do not suppress your feelings. While learning what not to do as a result of your upbringing, you also will learn of your good qualities. You are personable, you are bright, you are a high achiever, and you are a caring and honest person. Make the most of these qualities.

Understand your parents for who they are. When possible, let their bad actions go. Forgive them (not excusing them) by understanding what may have driven their actions. Your parents' personalities will not dictate the type of person you will become. Remove all blame for the incest incidents from yourself. That will be your mother's action, not yours; you own no part of it.

Do not let the actions and deeds of the past control your future. Have confidence that you are strong enough to lead a life you will be proud of. Do not hide or avoid your feelings. In spite of your past, strive to be a loving person. Do not be afraid. There will be others in your life who will love you for who you are.

You will survive. In fact, you will thrive. Know

that people like me will be there for you whenever needed.

Your older self,

Max

* * *

As I finished, I looked at each of them. Feeling like I had beat them all up, I attempted to acknowledge that I too had been guilty of bad conduct.

When I was finished, the Arbiter asked if I was done.

I thought for a while as I looked at the three individuals standing before me.

"Sir, I think the one thing I would like to do is to offer my sincere forgiveness to my mother and the others and, in turn, ask for their forgiveness."

Victor and Ed smiled, acknowledging my request and their acceptance.

Mom raised her head, smiled, and reached out as if to give me a hug.

None of them spoke.

Encouraged by what had happened, I asked the Arbiter if I could ask a few questions. We then talked about a number of subjects. This was without accusation and almost felt like a happy discussion. There was no blame or animosity between any of us. The fact that Victor had been an alcoholic, my mother had incestuous encounters, and Ed was frivolous about almost everything did not matter.

It was interesting that Victor and Ed seemed to be aware of all the issues my mother and I had. She was a complex lady, and I think we all knew that. There was laughing, joking, and stories of remembrance. It was as though we all had warts, including me, and it didn't matter. We were just a family.

Near the end of the discussion, we again talked about the forgiveness we had for each other. We promised to talk again soon. Ed even wanted to discuss the upcoming Super Bowl. He had been a Minnesota Viking fan and wanted to know how they were doing. As they walked off arm in arm and began to fade from sight, they were all talking with each other and laughing—even Mom.

A strange feeling came over me. I felt no hatred. It was gone! The feeling was so liberating and what I had sought for so long. The loss of the feelings of hatred had occurred so fast it was like flipping a light switch: one second, they were there, the next they were gone.

It was the Martin Luther King Jr. feeling—Free at last!

I sat in the attic clutching my pillow and tried to take in what had just occurred. I could not explain it, but I was suddenly free. The experience was not logical. My engineer brain had trouble with that. I'm not sure if it was a spiritual experience or not, but it was real to me. What's more, the experience seemed like it had freed my mom, dad, and Ed too.

Now to open those boxes.

I tore into the boxes without hesitation. They contained a treasure trove of personal history. There were several baby books with thorough entries, clothes I'd worn, toys, pictures, letters, trophies, and other memorabilia. Mom had saved my Hopalong Cassidy drinking cup from the 1950s. I even found some old letters from Victor when he was in WWII. There were even letters and cards from Beth, Anne, and the other kids.

Claudia had told me that Mom did not recognize Beth and those kids, but Mom had saved their cards and letters. Maybe Mom was not so against my family as Claudia would have liked me to think.

The item that surprised me most was a rolled-up tube of yellowed paper. It was the coloring scroll Lissie had given me so many years before. Unrolling it part way, I saw a partially colored-in horse and wagon. The feelings of love and excitement I'd felt the day she gave it to me came flooding back.

My mother had done a wonderful job of tracking my childhood. It would take hours and hours to explore the contents of these boxes. I looked forward to the task. These things were too valuable to remain in the attic. They would have a prominent place in my home.

When I climbed down the rickety attic stairs just over an hour after climbing them, I felt lighter. I felt free of hatred and guilt, and I felt a sense of belonging that I'd never felt in my life.

* * *

After moving the boxes to my office in the house, I went back to the garage, put my leathers on, and started the hog.

Riding out of town and breathing the clean air and feeling the sunshine, I realized how fortunate I was to have had that encounter. How fortunate I was to achieve forgiveness, and how fortunate I was to be rid of the hatred.

Then the tears came. Not a tear when Victor died, not a tear at Ed's grave, and never a tear for Mom.

But now, as I rode down that highway, the tears came. And it felt wonderful.

"Forgiveness does not change the past,

but it does enlarge the future."

Ed Boese[2]

Acknowledgements

First, I would like to thank my family. Without their interest and support, this book would not have become a reality.

This book was not a quick task but rather a lengthy endeavor that required almost four years to write. Part of the reason it took so long was that the subject matter was so upsetting.

I could not have completed the book without the help of numerous people. It was Stacy Ennis (an editor and published author in her own right) who helped me develop the format and story line for the book. Stacy also brought Donna Cook (an editor and published author) in to critique our outline. Then it was up to me to write the book following that outline.

During this process I engaged Cristen Iris, a substantive editor extraordinaire. Without Cristen's attention to detail and style, this book would not have been finished.

I also appreciate the many readers who provided comments and proofreading along the way: Stephanie Hendrixson, Sandy Matherly, Dianne Ruxton, and Suzanne Mathis.

I would be remiss not to mention Robert Sweesy for his publishing services.

Sources

1 King, Martin Luther, Jr., BrainyQuote. Updated 2019.

https://www.brainyquote.com/quotes/martin_luther_king_jr_101472?src=t_forgiveness

2 Boese, Ed. PassItOn.com. Updated February 7, 2019.

https://www.passiton.com/inspirational-quotes/3128-forgiveness-does-not-change-the-past-but-it